WARRIORS
OF THE RAVEN

Alan Gibbons is a full time writer and a visiting speaker and lecturer at schools, colleges and literary events nationwide, including the major book festivals. He lives in Liverpool with his wife and four children.

Alan Gibbons has twice been shortlisted for the Carnegie Medal, with *The Edge* and *Shadow of the Minotaur* (the first book in the Legendeer trilogy), which also won the 'Book I Couldn't Put Down' category of the Blue Peter Book Awards.

Warriors of the Raven is the final part of the Legendeer Trilogy.

Also by Alan Gibbons

THE LEGENDEER TRILOGY
Shadow of the Minotaur
Vampyr Legion
Warriors of the Raven

Blood Pressure
Caught in the Crossfire
Chicken
The Dark Beneath
The Defender
The Edge
Ganging Up
Hold On
Julie and Me . . . and Michael Owen Makes Three
Julie and Me: Treble Trouble
The Lost Boys' Appreciation Society
Playing with Fire
Whose Side Are You On?

WARRIORS
OF THE RAVEN

ALAN GIBBONS

Orion
Children's Books

First published in Great Britain in 2001
as a Dolphin paperback
This paperback edition published 2006
by Orion Children's Books
a division of the Orion Publishing Group Ltd
Orion House
5 Upper St Martin's Lane
London WC2H 9EA

The Orion Publishing Group's policy is to use papers that are natural,
renewable and recyclable products and made from wood grown is
sustainable forests. The logging and manufacturing processses are expected
to conform to the environmental regulations of the country of origin.

A catalogue record for this is available
from the British Library

Printed in Great Britain by
Clays Ltd, St Ives plc.

ISBN-10   1 84255 001 2
ISBN-13   978 1 84255 001 4

www.orionbooks.co.uk

The Mischief-Maker

He could feel them boring into him. They were like diamonds, brilliant but sparkling with malice, the Mischief-Maker's eyes flashing in the far shadows of the firelit hall.

He hates me.

It hardly mattered. The boy thought he was invincible.

Nothing can harm me.

Legend made it so.

He was the bright prince, favourite of the gods of Asgard. No sword could cut him, no axe lay him low, no spear pierce his flesh. This was the great gift Fate had given him. He could feel his strength coursing through his veins like a stream of molten iron.

Nothing can hurt me.

He met the Mischief-Maker's eyes, yellow and unblinking, like a wolf's.

Not even you.

'Ready for your test?' said a gruff voice.

He looked in the direction of Odin, greatest of the gods, read encouragement in the All-father's one eye, and nodded.

Do your worst.

And they did. Every warrior of Asgard took his turn. They launched a hail of javelins but they bounced off the boy like raindrops. Some flung stones but they fell to the ground harmlessly, like dust. Others set about him with their swords, yet he was still not injured. The deadliest weapons came within hair's-breadth of him then glanced off, or simply clattered uselessly to the stone floor. It was as if he were protected by an invisible outer skin. He looked around proudly and smiled as the applause of god and hero alike echoed round the walls of Valhalla.

'Brave Balder,' said Odin. 'Because you are pure in heart neither javelin, nor stone, nor sword can hurt you.'

That's me, Balder the hero. I can't be harmed.

He smiled again, revelling in the praise, but something troubled him. It was yellow-eyed Loki, the Mischief-Maker. Where had he gone? It wasn't long before the boy discovered him whispering in a corner.

What are you talking about?

He was aware of Loki's nature. Wily, cunning, born to make mischief. He felt its hostile power in the marrow of his bones.

Nothing good or decent, that's for certain.

But there was no way of finding out what Loki was up to. He was too far away, and he had covered his mouth with his hand in order to hide his words.

I am invincible, so why am I afraid of you?

What trick have you got up your sleeve?

Odin's son Thor, the god of thunder, marched across the hall and handed the boy a huge drinking horn, filled to the brim.

'Drain it in one, young Balder,' he roared.

The boy looked around and saw the gods cheering him on. He looked into the horn of mead and grinned.

'All right, I will.'

And he raised the horn to his lips and started to drink.

'Drink, drink, drink,' chanted the gods of Asgard.

He could feel the intoxicating mead spilling down his chin and onto the front of his tunic.

'Drink, drink, drink.'

His senses started to swim but he was determined to finish it. In this hall the boy could become a man. At last he had drained

4

it right to the bottom. His cheeks were on fire, and the walls seemed to spin. A rich, comforting heat swept through him, making him want to laugh out loud.

'This mead is strong stuff,' he said.

His words brought a roar of approval.

'Hear that? The lad likes his honeyed drink.'

'It is strong indeed,' said Thor. 'But not as strong as our young prince. He stands up to our weapons as if they were mere toys.'

'That's what they are,' he agreed. 'Toys.'

The thunderer clapped him on the shoulder.

'Listen to him, he calls our weapons toys. Will nobody else try his hand against Balder the invincible?'

The boy was laughing, both at the words and at the effects of the mead, but the smile faded as his eyes fell once more on the lean, prowling form of Loki. The Evil One had sidled up to blind Hodur and was whispering in his ear.

I recognize this.

It was foretold in the legends. Hodur has a role in Balder's downfall.

***My** downfall.*

But what was the prophecy? What danger could sightless Hodur pose?

I am charmed against injury.

What can a blind man do to me?

They had played the game of weapons and he had won against all comers. But life is never without risk.

Every game has that one unsettling rule that can turn the whole thing on its head, the trick, the twist, just like the joker in a pack of cards. How did the prophecy go? By neither metal nor stone can Balder be injured. But there was more to the prophecy.

I have to remember.

But the drink was dulling his senses.

There's more. What's the joker in the pack? How does it go?

He could see Loki whispering in Hodur's ear, encouraging him to do something. He saw the narrow, wolfish eyes and wondered what the Evil One had in store. Then Hodur was stringing his bow.

That's it.

I've discovered the joker.

I know what it is!

Mistletoe.

Balder was invincible against all things. All but one.

All things save the mistletoe!

Suddenly the drink was a curse. The thrill of its taste, the warmth it had spread through his body, he couldn't enjoy them any more. It was its other effects he felt. His movements were slow, his legs were unsteady, his words were slurred. He wanted to shout out, to yell a warning.

It isn't a game any more.

He's going to kill me.

The boy saw Loki's murderous eyes and he opened his mouth. But the words wouldn't come.

'What's that, Balder?' asked Thor.

'Speak slowly,' said Odin. 'I can't understand you.'

But he could do nothing. He saw Hodur's arrow nocked on the bowstring and at last he understood. That's what Loki had been planning. Poor, blind Hodur. The only one present who would be unable to see Loki's trickery. The Evil One had handed him a mistletoe twig shaped like an arrow, the deadly arrow of pain.

'All part of the game,' Loki hissed, no longer caring to hide his words.

The boy's lips formed a protest.

'N-no.'

It's no game.

But his words came out in a slurred mumble.

6

'What's that?' asked Thor. 'Speak up, brave Balder.'

He couldn't speak up. He couldn't explain himself and he couldn't defend himself. Encouraged by Loki, Hodur had drawn the bowstring back to his ear. In his ignorance, the blind man thought it was mere sport, all part of the game, one more harmless attack like the javelins, the stones and the swords. Amid the carousing and laughter, Hodur allowed his aim to be guided by Loki. A cunning smile filled the Evil One's face.

'No.'

The string stretched back and even amid the noise in the hall, he could hear the creak of the bow. The deadly shaft was aimed straight at his heart. At last terror wrenched a cry from his lips.

'NO!'

Jon Jonsson flew across the room, propelling himself away from the arrow, a hand flung across his chest in a protective gesture.

'What's got into you?' said an anxious voice. 'It's only a game.'

Jon didn't answer. He was too busy tearing off the mask and gloves and yanking leads out of computer sockets. He saw his father and he felt like crying out for sheer joy. He was back in the real world. The sense of relief was overwhelming.

'Jon?'

Jon. Not Balder. Jon. He was no longer playing a part, no longer caught up in the crazy game. This was his real self. He shook his head. He was beginning to recover from the fright the game had given him.

'It's OK,' he said. 'I'm OK.'

He started giggling fit to burst. Though his senses were clearing, he was still feeling the effects of the mead. Besides, he was on the edge of hysteria.

'It's a game. That's all it is, a game.'

'Of course it's a game,' his father said. 'I'm the one who designed it, remember?'

Dad was staring at him, the clear-blue eyes riveted to his. But the stern look didn't bother Jon. Nothing could faze him now, not after Loki's evil glare.

'It's unbelievable,' said Jon. 'So real. It was as though I was actually there. I wasn't me in there. I wasn't *playing* Balder. I was him.'

His father's expression relaxed.

'Now *that*'s something I'm pleased to hear,' he said. 'It's got to be a totally convincing experience. You really like it?'

Jon hesitated.

'Well?'

'I'm not sure like is quite the right word,' he replied. 'I was scared witless. But it blew me away. What a rush!'

'Go on,' Dad said. 'Tell me what you mean by that. Exactly. This game has got to work. Our future depends on it.'

Jon nodded. He remembered the day Dad got the job working for Magna-com. He had danced round the living room like a madman, waving the letter in triumph.

'The most successful, innovative computer-game company in the world,' he had cried. 'And they want me to help design their new game.'

Jon knew all about Magna-com, of course. What teenage boy didn't? He had the first two parts of the *Legendeer* series, *Shadow of the Minotaur* and *Vampyr Legion*.

They'd been his Christmas and birthday presents. He'd marvelled at the graphics, shuddered at the realism of the monsters. Now here was Dad, *his* dad, given the responsibility of taking *The Legendeer* forward to new heights. The next game was going to use all this Virtual Reality stuff. Magna-com had postponed its introduction twice. Production difficulties, they said. Jon picked up the mask and gloves, then ran his hands over the skintight black suit he was wearing. The ultimate accessories for the ultimate game. What was the advertising angle? Yes: *The Game You Really Get Into*. These were the things that were going to blow away the opposition and make *Legendeer 3: Warriors of the Raven* the hottest computer game ever.

'Virtual Reality,' Jon murmured, still able to taste the mead on his lips. 'The ultimate game.'

'Parallel Reality,' his father said, correcting him.

'I beg your pardon?'

'Parallel Reality, that's what Magna-com calls it. It's a step beyond Virtual Reality. You're not just seeing your surroundings. This is a complete multisensory experience. You touch your surroundings, smell them, taste them. This thing you're wearing is a PR suit. It makes the illusion possible.'

Jon didn't care what it was called. The sensation was amazing. Once he was inside the suit, the world of the Norse gods had come alive. He had smelt the logs burning in the great hall of Valhalla, he had heard the hiss of the warriors' swords leaving their scabbards, he had felt the fire's heat, most of all he had tasted the mead. For the first time in his life he had actually been drunk! And all with his parents' permission too. The one sobering thought occurred to him when he looked down at his wrist. He was wearing a gizmo rather like a watch. It was his points bracelet, and it registered a big, fat zero. He'd entered the red zone. Red for failure, red for blood. The price of being the target of a mistletoe arrow.

'I lost,' he said.

'You lost,' his father told him, 'because you panicked. You allowed yourself to believe the illusion. The secret of winning is to keep cool, to know the limits of the game.'

Jon glanced at the monitor screen. The screen-save had kicked in, a flurry of numbers, threes, sixes and nines.

'You'd have panicked too,' he said. 'That arrow of mistletoe.

9

It's in the rules. It's the one thing that can hurt me. And Loki, what a villain. Those eyes. How did you get them like that? The way he looked at me, it made my flesh creep.'

'That's the general idea,' said his father. 'Magna-com **want** you spooked right down to the tips of your toes. That**'s the** buzz. It's like a horror film. If it doesn't take you to the **edge of** your seat, you feel cheated. Their games promise a **white-**knuckle ride. That's the big selling point. You feel you're there. We daren't disappoint our audience. It's not all down to me, of course. Magna-com have a whole team of programmers and designers working on the game. I'm not sure who came up with the eyes.'

'You mean you haven't met the rest of the team?'

'I haven't even spoken to them.'

'You're kidding!'

'No, that's how Magna-com works. Each of its designers and programmers has been working alone on one tiny part of the whole game. I got level eight: *Balder and the Arrow*, and the last two levels, *Warriors of the Raven* and *Ragnarok*. At least, I collaborated on them. Working this way is like painting one piece of a jigsaw without seeing the whole picture. Top-secret stuff. I suppose that's how they stop their competitors catching up with them.'

Jon peeled off the PR suit.

'There is one drawback though.'

His father's face fell. The game was about to hit the shops.

'What's that?'

'I'm not sure I want another go. My stomach is turning over at the thought of it. That's how scary it was.'

He remembered the arrow pointing at his heart, the one thing that could kill the hero Balder, and he felt the rush again, an adrenaline burst of horror.

'It gets a lot scarier,' said his father. 'The Balder episode comes just before the big finale. Level nine is when the forces of good and evil line up. But just you wait till you get to level ten. That's Ragnarok, the final battle. The Norse gods, led by Odin, descend from Asgard to battle the forces of darkness. It's got demons, dragons, zombies, streams of fire, earthquakes, mass slaughter. End-of-the-world stuff. We're talking Armageddon.'

'Not sure how I'll handle that,' said Jon. 'Scarier than the Balder level, you say?'

'Much scarier. Balder is dead, or at least living on as a ghost, so the player becomes Heimdall, the watchman of the gods and arch-enemy of the evil Loki. You have to warn them of the coming evil and summon them from Asgard to fight the final battle.'

The promise of excitement got the better of Jon.

'Can I have a go at it?' he asked, just about overcoming his fear of the game. 'This Ragnarok level?'

'You'll have to wait a while before you can get onto the final levels,' Dad replied. 'You have to complete this one first.'

Jon looked disappointed.

'You will play again though, won't you? I'm relying on you for the teen angle. You're my guinea pig.'

Jon remembered the feeling of invincibility, the forbidden sensation of being drunk. No way would he get that feeling any other time. His parents were strict about that sort of thing. No doubt about it, he was already itching to go again. Maybe if he continued to trial it, he'd get a shot at the other levels. *Warriors of the Raven* was certainly addictive. The fright he had felt as Hodur aimed his arrow was already fading. He winked at his father.

'Just you try and stop me.'

BOOK ONE

The Book of the Legendeer

1

That same evening, many miles away, another teenage boy was making his way through the trembling, drizzly darkness of a mid-February evening. Watching him, you might be forgiven for thinking he was being followed, pursued even, such was his haste. Phoenix Graves was heading home from a friend's house. At fourteen, he was the same age as Jon Jonsson, as dark and sallow as the other boy was pale and blond. Phoenix owed his looks to his Greek ancestry, on his mother's side. His family had only been in England for three generations. Up to this point, however, though there were many similarities in their lives, Phoenix didn't even know of Jon's existence. But that was about to change. He had played *The Legendeer* just as Jon had. He had been the very first player in fact, a guinea pig for his own father, the first man to work on the game. Like Jon, he had seen the threes, sixes and nines spiralling on the screen, and wondered what they meant. He had worn the PR suit and been hooked up to the computer. He had been sucked into its terrifying worlds, forced to face its demons. But there was a difference. Jon still thought *The Legendeer* was entertainment, fun. Phoenix knew better. He knew what lay behind the marketing and the graphics, and it haunted his dreams. You didn't play this game. It played you. Here, on this lonely street, he was already bracing himself for the night. With night came dreams, and with those dreams came terror. Soon he and Jon would meet, and at that

15

crossroads in time and place their lives would be turned upside down.

The trill of a mobile phone rippled through the damp air.

'Hello?' said Phoenix, pulling it from his blazer pocket. 'Oh, hi, Mum. Something wrong?'

'Only a son who was meant to be home over an hour ago,' she replied frostily. 'Where have you been till this time – Laura's?'

'That's right, I phoned Dad to ask if I could go round to hers after school. Didn't he pass on the message?'

Mum's impatience fairly crackled through the air.

'We're talking about your dad. He's out. No note though.'

'I did tell him. Honest.'

The voice at the other end softened.

'I know. It's not your fault, Phoenix. Where are you, by the way?'

'By the bank in the High Street. I'll be with you in ten minutes.'

'See you then.'

Phoenix slipped the mobile back in his pocket and shook his head.

'Dad! Can't you get anything right?'

At that moment he glimpsed his reflection in a shop window. Seeing himself rendered faint and ghostly by the darkness, he was overwhelmed by memories. Phoenix was a boy who had his demons. They perched on the cusp of his memory, waded through the murky backwaters of his dreams. They had their claws in him and they were never going to let go. Just a little further on, he came face to face with one of those demons. A poster was displayed on a notice board outside Brownleigh police station.

STEVEN ADAMS, 14.
DO YOU KNOW THE WHEREABOUTS
OF THIS BOY?

Phoenix read the details. Steve Adams. He was the boy who'd been his tormentor at school and had followed him into the terrifying world of the game. He had not returned. Missing since the autumn, the poster said. If only they knew. Phoenix read right to the end. Not that he was going to learn anything new. He knew the whole thing by heart. What's more, he knew exactly where Adams was. But it wasn't the kind of information he could share with the police. Their jurisdiction didn't stretch that far.

Five minutes later, Phoenix was home.

'Mum?'

She emerged from the living room.

'Is he . . . ?'

'If you're after Dad, he walked in the moment I put the phone down. Not a word of apology for forgetting to tell me where you were, of course.'

Phoenix rolled his eyes. That was the old man. Only one thing on his mind. A game called *The Legendeer*. Mind you, with the stakes as high as they were, he could hardly be blamed for being obsessed.

'And yes, before you ask, he is in the study.'

Phoenix dropped his bag in the hallway and joined his father in the cramped, cluttered room. There had to be order in the chaotic piles of books and notepads, but it defeated Phoenix. The latest stack was all about the Viking legends. A torrent of publicity had announced that the new *Legendeer* would be based on them. It was called *Warriors of the Raven*. After the Greek myths and the gothic world of vampires and were-wolves, it was a logical choice. Phoenix flicked through one volume, pausing at an illustration of the evil Loki. The Norse myths had been unfamiliar to him, but he was rapidly becoming an expert. The gods of Asgard on the one hand, Loki and his legions of hell on the other.

'Anything?'

17

'Give me a moment.'

Phoenix had asked the question more in hope than expectation. He wasn't surprised when John Graves gave a shake of the head.

'A couple of accidental hits on our website. Just random surfers mostly, and a couple of boys looking for the official Magna-com website. Nothing to help us though. I don't know what to do next.'

He shoved his chair back on its castors and eased into the headrest, closing his eyes. He'd been chasing shadows for weeks and it showed.

'I had high hopes of the website. I thought it would stir up a little interest from somebody. Looks like it's just another dead end. It will be a disaster if the game goes on sale but there doesn't seem to be any way to stop it happening.'

'We can't give up,' Phoenix protested, hearing the resignation in Dad's voice.

'I don't intend to,' said Dad. 'I was the first programmer to work on it, I kind of started all this. So don't you worry, I intend to finish it. But I will admit I'm starting to feel discouraged. I've been trying to find out who they got to take over my old job for months now.'

John Graves had been as delighted as Jon Jonsson's father when he was asked to develop *The Legendeer*. But delight had soon turned to horror. Now he was a thorn in Magna-com's side.

'I've tried every contact I know . . . *twice*. I tell you, whoever Magna-com got to finish *The Legendeer* this time, they're not in this country.'

'What makes you say that?'

'Because I must have talked to every single programmer and designer based here. Want to see our phone bill? The company must have moved the project abroad, out of our reach.'

Phoenix glanced at the PC.

'So what do we do?'

Dad shook his head.

'I've read everything on the Norse legends and every computer game and website you can imagine. Nothing. The launch date is just round the corner. Let me sleep on it, son. I'm all out of ideas. I necd time to think.'

Phoenix sighed. Time was just what they didn't have. Did he have to remind Dad what came to him every night? Demons, hundreds of them, all knocking on a virtual door. Demanding entry to this world.

'Have you forgotten what we're dealing with?'

Their eyes fell on the computer games in the corner, then on the Parallel Reality suits. Finally, there were the folders full of cuttings, the fragments of a tale of menace.

They had been the first to understand what *The Legendeer* was all about. Not illusion, but a different, menacing reality. Not entertainment, but horror.

'It's more than a game, Dad. It's a plague. We've got to find a way to stop it.'

'Phoenix,' said Dad wearily, 'I haven't forgotten anything. I want to put an end to this as much as you do. I just don't know how to. For the first time I actually feel like I'm on the losing side.'

Seeing the expression of defeat in his father's eyes, Phoenix lowered his voice.

'Sorry, I'm frustrated because we don't seem to be getting anywhere.'

Dad smiled.

'You and me both.'

Phoenix looked out at the yew trees in the back garden. For a fleeting instant he thought he saw somebody watching from the lane. But he'd felt that way ever since he first played *The Legendeer*. If he could look into their nightmare world, they

19

were quite capable of looking out at him. Phoenix couldn't turn his back without sensing the terror at his shoulder.

'What are you looking at?' Dad asked.

Phoenix continued to stare, as if trying to peel away the darkness, layer by layer.

'I beg your pardon? Oh, nothing. Just my mind playing tricks.'

But it was more than that. It was the shadow of his demons.

Phoenix was in a room. There were brilliant white walls – so white it was hard to keep his eyes open – and a black carpet and curtains. Against the far wall somebody was sitting with his back to Phoenix, working on a computer.

'Who are you?' Phoenix asked.

'Don't you know?' came the reply.

Phoenix recognized the voice immediately and retreated to the door.

'No,' he said. 'It can't be.'

The chair swivelled round and a familiar pair of eyes met his.

'Surprise surprise.'

Phoenix saw a teenage boy, the boy from the police-station poster. At least the face was that of a fourteen-year-old boy. The body was muscular and powerful beyond his years.

'Adams!'

Steve Adams grinned. He held up a copy of *The Legendeer, Part Three*. Phoenix focused on the new title *Warriors of the Raven*. It was only then, as he stared at the illustrations on the case, that Phoenix became aware of a second presence, barely visible at all. Adams was threatening enough, but this second presence, the one that pulled his strings, was pure evil. He was there all right, the force behind *The Legendeer*, the Games-master. He was playing Adams the way a puppeteer plays his marionette.

'Coming out to play?' asked Adams, rising to his feet.

The hands that reached out towards Phoenix seemed to be dissolving and disintegrating as they came closer. The flesh bubbled and cracked open, scraps of greying skin peeling away and dropping to the floor. A new face was taking shape beneath the old. Serpents were sprouting from the head, writhing and twisting above grotesque eyes and mouth.

In an instant, the image had changed. A vampire's fangs flashed and dripped venom. Finally there was a new face, framed by hair as red as flame and wicked eyes that flashed yellow. They were burning into him with a hatred beyond human imagining.

'No!' yelled Phoenix, shrinking back. 'No, no, no.'

He woke up, dripping with sweat. His demons were coming out of the darkness.

2

Jon tracked his father down to the bottom of the garden. He walked gingerly on the frozen ground. Dad was wielding a huge, long-handled hammer, smashing away at the wall of a crumbling brick outhouse.

'It's time for the game,' said Jon, clapping his gloveless hands together against the cold.

Dad consulted his watch.

'That time already. This is taking longer than I'd expected. The condition it was in, I thought it might fall down by itself.'

'What are you going to do with it?'

'If I can manage to demolish it, I'm going to have a self-contained study room built out here, using the old foundations. No phone, no distractions.'

He wiped his face with a handkerchief and leaned the hammer against the wall. Jon seized on it immediately, swinging it round his head.

'Hey, watch that thing,' said Dad.

'Don't you see?' said Jon. 'I'm Thor the mighty thunder god and this is Mjollnir my magic hammer.'

'There's a safer way to be a Viking hero,' said Dad. 'Let's play the game. You're a lucky lad. Everybody else has got a few more days to wait.'

Jon nodded eagerly. He had been waiting for this moment all day. What if he could complete the whole thing before anybody in school even had the chance to buy a copy? He led the way indoors. As he stepped into the PR suit and pulled it up, feeling the material clinging to him, he had mixed emotions. The thrill of expectation was combined with a sense of horror.

'Are you OK, Jon?' his father asked, handing him the mask and gloves, already hooked up to the PC.

'Fine.'

But there was no disguising the shake in his voice.

'That scary, huh?'

Jon nodded. His throat was dry. A question popped into his head:

What next after death?

'Dad?' he asked, feeling the mask snap over his jawline. 'How does this Balder story turn out, anyway?'

'In the old Viking legend, do you mean, or in the computer game?'

'Both.'

'Well, in the legend, Balder dies. It's the incident that leads to the final conflict between good and evil.'

'*He dies?*'

'Uh huh. The evil Loki tricks blind Hodur into slaying him. It is the event which leads to the day of reckoning, Ragnarok. Some call it the twilight of the gods. That's what the whole game is leading up to, a massive showdown between the gods of Asgard and the forces of darkness.'

'But that spoils the whole game. How am I supposed to win if I'm dead? That's stupid.'

'I think you're missing the point about computer games, Jon. It's up to the player. The story on which it is based is just a starting point. You rewrite the legend yourself. Computer games take all sorts of liberties with the original stories. Within the rules of the game, anything's possible. It's my job to make kids believe they can conquer huge monsters. Look, if you want a crack at the top levels, you've got to stop putting it off and get past this one.'

Jon nodded, but he still didn't like the sound of it: Balder dies!

He listened to the reassuring purr of the PC and strapped on the last piece of Legendeer apparatus, the points bracelet.

'Ready or not,' he said defiantly, 'here I come.'

The credits rolled and three ancient women appeared, cloaked in grey robes. They acted as guides through *Warriors of the Raven*.

'Welcome to the world of *The Legendeer*,' they chorused. 'We three sisters are the Norns. We are creatures of the past, the present and the future. We spin the fates of men and women. We pave the path you tread through life, to Asgard on high . . . or to foul Hel below.'

Jon felt his breath catch as the sisters beckoned him on.

'Our story begins in glorious Asgard itself, home of the gods. You will play the part of young Balder, noblest and greatest in spirit of those who dwell within its impenetrable walls. He is loved by man and god alike. As a result of his fame, he is hated by the Mischief-Maker, that most evil of spirits, wily Loki.'

Jon gritted his teeth. As bad guys went, this Loki was *bad*. The Norns led him to a jutting horn of rock, from which he could see the whole of the strange world of the Norse gods. Stretching out beneath the white sky was a plain ringed by bare, rugged hills. The snow lay in thick drifts below him. But hanging motionless before him was the most curious feature of the entire vista, a frozen rainbow that arched glistening into the sky. He had set foot on it before, the first time he had played, but he still marvelled at it. It was unlike any rainbow he had ever seen, opaque and sparkling like frost. Even that wasn't all. In the glittering light, as if through a window, he could see the vastness of space.

Prepare to have your mind blown, he thought.

'Behold,' the Norns continued, 'the path called Bifrost. On the other side of this rainbow bridge you will find Asgard, and within its walls Valhalla where the fallen heroes carouse for all eternity.'

Milky wreaths of stars, planets and blazing comets flashed in the brightness of the rainbow. But, as still and monumental as it stood, Jon could almost feel the tension in the sparkling arch. It was like a groaning giant, desperate to unburden itself and crash to earth. In the furthest distance, half-lost in the snow-glare of the distant hills, he could see something else. The palace of Asgard. He remembered the huge, studded doors, soaring turrets and glistening roofs from his first go on the game.

'In this journey through the Northland,' the Norns went on, 'you will relive the fate of Balder, then of Heimdall, watchman of the gods. To win, you must blow the Gjall horn and summon them for their final battle with the Evil One and his demon army. As Heimdall you have an awesome responsibility. You are the one who must slay the demon-master Loki himself. Are you ready to begin?'

'Ready,' said Jon.

And so his second game began. He crossed the rainbow bridge and entered Asgard. He was hailed as Balder and accepted the challenge of the weapons. He felt his own invincibility, the sensation of the mead inflaming his senses, the terror as Loki guided blind Hodur's aim with the bow. He glanced at his points bracelet. He had a healthy score.

This time I won't panic.

He could feel the effect of the mead, but he kept his concentration. The score on his points bracelet climbed.

This time I'm going to win.

I'm going on to the next level.

He saw Loki whispering in Hodur's ear. Then, ever so slowly, and with murderous intent, the bow was aimed at his chest. The effect of the mead was becoming stronger.

Got to think, to stay alert.

Easier said than done. His mind was getting fogged. He could feel the vibration of the points bracelet as his score started to fall.

I won't shout out.

I won't ask for help.

I'll just jump out of the way.

But he was unable to move, never mind jump. He was rooted to the spot, paralysed by the effects of the mead. The bowstring went taut, then the arrow was loosed.

There was a sickening thud, an impact that threatened to rearrange his insides, and he was falling, falling, the room spinning and darkening around him. He could hear his father's voice, as if from far away.

'Jon, what's wrong?'

He could feel his father's fingers on his face. He was going to remove the mask and break the game's spell.

'No,' he said. 'Don't.'

The words came back to him, the ones that had come to mind earlier.

What next after death?

But he wasn't dead at all, not really. He could see and hear. There was more to learn from the game.

'I'm all right,' he said stubbornly. 'I don't need any help.'

Then his father's voice and touch drew away, as if fading into the far distance, and Jon was once more part of the game.

What's happening to me?

What kind of game is this?

'Ready to continue your journey?' said a voice. 'Ready to take the final step, to go beyond illusion into another world?'

He found himself standing on the deck of a ship.

'Where am I?'

On the prow of the ship stood the Norns, the three dark-veiled sisters. Around them the sea appeared to be on fire. Flaming arrows filled the sky above them.

'Why, this is your funeral ship, Balder.'

'Funeral ship? Am I dead?'

'For the purposes of the game, yes. But the game goes on. The game is without end. You are not just one hero, intrepid player. You are *all* heroes. Remember, if you take up the challenge, you will play the part of Heimdall. You will blow the Gjall horn and summon the gods to the final battle. Do you dare?'

Jon's mind was working overtime. You die and you can still win? This was the weirdest game he had ever played.

'Behold,' said the Norns. 'The gods of Asgard bid Balder farewell. But their anger turns against Loki. They see his tearless eyes and they know he is the guilty one.'

The ship began to sail, drifting through banks of thick fog. Then the mists started to clear.

'Behold,' said the Norns, pointing the way. 'This is the Mischief-Maker's fate, his punishment for the death of Balder.'

Loki was being dragged down steep stairs in an underground cavern. All the way he was shouting and cursing his captors.

'Unhand me,' he shrieked. 'It wasn't me. Hodur did it.'

'Yes,' said Thor. 'Hodur shot the arrow, but you guided his hand. Yours is the crime, Loki.'

'This is the gulf of Black Grief,' the Norns explained. 'Here the Evil One will lie bound in chains on three sharp-edged rocks. Above him is fastened a giant serpent. Venom drips from its jaws and will fall for all time upon Loki's face. This is the punishment for the Mischief-Maker's crime.'

Jon watched fascinated yet horrified as Loki twisted and writhed, struggling to avoid the poison. He witnessed the Mischief-Maker's torment, heard his screams.

'His anger will grow. It will fester and turn against all

27

mankind. Every moment of every day he lies tormented here, he will plot his revenge. Above all he will blame you. One day those chains will break and the Evil One will walk free once more. Make yourself ready for that day of vengeance, player, for on that day of Ragnarok you will surely have to face him again.'

Jon saw Loki's head turn and the yellow eyes fixed him with a look of utter hatred, a loathing that seemed to set the air alight. He recoiled, horror piercing his heart more effectively than any arrow. Ahead of him he saw something golden, a kind of portal of shimmering light.

'Step through,' said the Norns. 'Cross the threshold and you will no longer be playing, but *living* the game. That's right, enter the game's embrace. We are offering you a world beyond your wildest imagining.'

Jon looked into the light and felt his heart lurch. He could see shadows, the hidden shapes of strange creatures. There was a pain in his chest and his mind was haunted by Loki's yellow eyes. No, he wouldn't go into the light. He wished he had let Dad remove the mask. Something was wrong.

Very wrong.

'That's it,' he said, pulling at the mask of the PR suit. 'This is just too weird. I've had enough.'

But the game wasn't ready to let him go just yet. The mask clung to him, tugging at his face as if it was going to peel away his skin. He clawed at the skintight mask, but still it wouldn't budge.

'Dad, help me!'

Two pairs of hands were tugging at it now. For a moment, Jon could actually feel his skin beginning to tear from his face. Thousands of fragile strings seemed on the verge of snapping inside his flesh.

There was only one thought in his mind now. To escape from the game.

To be free of it.

'I don't want to be Balder,' he cried. 'I don't want to be Heimdall either. And I don't want your stupid challenge. Game over. Game over NOW!'

3

Phoenix turned his key in the lock. Laura Osibona followed him to the living room, giving the study a quick glance. She was his best friend. She knew his secret. She was always aware of it, the unremarkable boxroom where it had all started, where something as seemingly harmless as a computer game had turned into a nightmare. She thought of the menace that buzzed through the computer's hard drive and the monitor screen that had been transformed into a window onto horror.

'So what's the next move?' she asked.

'Good question,' Phoenix replied, dropping his school bag on the floor by the couch. 'Dad's completely stumped. Me too. The game is about to go on sale and we can't get anyone to listen to us. Still no news on the designer either. We know nothing about it except that it's about to hit the shops.'

'And that it's evil,' said Laura.

Laura had been part of it from the very beginning. Phoenix's partner in a two-player game. She had worn the PR suit and entered it alongside him. She had become aware of the malicious power that, unknown to either of them, was stealing into Jon Jonsson's life.

'I'm sure we'll get a lead somehow,' said Laura. 'After all, he's only . . .'

Her voice trailed off.

'Only human, is that what you were going to say? That's just it, Laura, Gamesmaster is simply a name we've given him. We don't know what he is. Come on,' said Phoenix. 'I'm going to see if our website has attracted any interest.'

'Legendeer.co.uk,' said Laura, reading the directory. 'Sounds like an official website.'

'That's the general idea,' said Phoenix.

They sat side by side at the work station, eyes fixed on the screen.

'Nothing,' Phoenix said disgustedly.

He shoved the mouse away.

'You'll find a way back into the game,' said Laura.

'You think so?'

'No,' said Laura. 'I *know* so. You will find a way back because you're not just another player. You're *the* player. That's what everything we have been through has taught us. You are the Legendeer.'

She was right. He was the one who had been at home there, among the demons and monsters. The same creatures that inhabited *The Legendeer* had haunted his dreams since early childhood. His whole life had been one long preparation for the game. Entering its world had been like coming home.

'For months I've felt like it was my destiny,' he said. 'But now . . . I have my doubts. Look, there's no connection any more. *Warriors of the Raven* is the hottest thing since colour tv, but we're still being kept at arm's length. We've no access to the new software.'

'But what about the numbers?' said Laura. 'To everybody else they were a mystery, just random figures on the screen. But you understood their importance. You knew they were the language of the game, its secret code.'

'That's just it, Laura. The numbers are the way in, but we don't even get them coming up on the screen any more. The Gamesmaster has shut us out. It's like nothing ever happened.'

'But it did happen,' Laura replied. 'It happened *to us*. We're not mad and we didn't make it up.'

She reached into a cardboard box next to her, and held up one of the Parallel Reality suits Phoenix's dad kept packed away.

'Remember this?'

'Of course I remember it,' said Phoenix.

The suit was how it had all begun. He remembered the skintight material pinching his flesh, the macabre sensation as it started binding with its skin, growing into it. He remembered the points bracelet blinking away, recording his score. Finally he remembered the shimmering golden portal, the gateway between the worlds.

'It's no accident that you were chosen to play,' said Laura. 'Your dad was the first to work on the game. Then there's Andreas . . .'

Phoenix closed his eyes. Andreas. He was the final part of the jigsaw, the reason that Phoenix was different from anyone else who had played the game. Andreas was his great-uncle. He was a man who had died years before Phoenix was born. Yet he was always in Phoenix's thoughts. And his dreams. It was the one thing that saved him from madness through all his adventures. No matter how terrible the menace that crouched in Phoenix's dreamworld, there was always Andreas in the distance, a comforting, ghostly presence, a secret speaker, a voice to guide him.

'It's like he's still alive sometimes,' Phoenix murmured. 'I hear him, here, in my mind.'

Andreas had been the first to enter the jaws of the nightmare. As a country schoolteacher in Greece, he had discovered that the demon world existed, the same world Phoenix had revisited in *The Legendeer*. He had given his life trying to warn people of the danger.

'You don't have to remind me of my destiny,' Phoenix said. 'I live with it every day. I know I have to beat the Gamesmaster. I know the terror that's waiting if I don't. But how do I get to him?'

32

Laura shrugged her shoulders.

'I only wish I knew. Anyway, show me this website of yours. I haven't seen it yet, remember?'

Phoenix brought it up on the screen, and Laura leaned forward.

'Well, those graphics ought to catch somebody's eye,' she said, mainly for Phoenix's benefit.

She watched the images from *Legendeer* Parts 1 and 2 crowding the screen: the Minotaur lumbering through the labyrinth, Medusa haunting the depths of her cave, Vampyrs lurking in the darkness. It was the stuff of fantasy to any surfer who came across the page, but it was memories to Phoenix and Laura. They'd been there. They'd faced those demons. It was real.

'I can't wait to see what you've put in it,' Laura said. 'What on earth did you say?'

Phoenix scrolled down.

'It wasn't easy. We didn't want to put anyone off by sounding like cranks. In the end, we decided to do it by asking questions.'

Laura's eyes roved over the page.

'What do you think?'

'I think it's very clever,' Laura replied. 'I just hope it's being read by the person that matters.'

The person that mattered was sitting on the floor of a room hundreds of miles away, kicking away the PR suit, and unfastening the points bracelet. He just wanted to get away.

'What happened?' asked Jon's father.

'That's it,' said Jon, his breath coming in sobs. 'I'm finished. I've had it with that stupid game.'

'But what's got you so upset?'

'What do you mean, what's got me upset? You were tugging at the mask, same as me. I thought I'd never get it off. I felt like I was going to be trapped in there. Besides . . .'

'Yes?'

'Dad, it's sick. I mean, *really* sick. What are you doing, getting involved in something like that?'

'Jon,' his father said patiently, 'just calm down and explain exactly what it is that's got you so spooked.'

'In a normal computer game,' Jon said, 'if you get killed you just go back to the start and begin again.'

'That's right,' said his father. 'And?'

'It's your game,' said Jon. 'You tell me. What's all this about the funeral ship, and Loki being tortured by poison? I mean, the look on his face. When he breaks free, I'm not going to be around to face him. It's like I'm being set up. The bad guy's going to come back and rip me to shreds.'

'Tell me about the funeral ship,' said his father.

'You know,' said Jon impatiently.

'No, Jon, I don't. It's completely new to me.'

'You mean you didn't write it into the game?'

'No.'

'Well, it's like this, I got hit by the arrow. Here.'

He touched his chest and winced. It actually hurt.

'Then it's like I'm a ghost. The Norns say I'm going to play again, I'm going to be some character called Heimdall.'

'That's right, Heimdall the watchman of the gods. He's the hero of level nine.'

'But they take me to this cave and show me what's happening to Loki. It's a torture chamber. You can hear him screaming. Then he looks at me and the Norns tell me that he'll break free one day. And guess what? When he does, he's going to come looking for me. Well, forget it. I'm not sticking around. Not the way he was looking at me.'

'Jon,' his father said, 'we are talking about a game, you know. OK, so somebody else on the team has added a new episode . . .'

'We're not just talking about an episode,' Jon protested

angrily. 'It's really sinister. I was standing there watching somebody getting tortured. I could see what the poison was doing to him. It just went on and on. You should have heard the screams. It was awful. And Loki's blaming *me* for it. If I go through the gateway, I won't ever come out.'

Jon had had enough. He wasn't even going to stay in the same room as the game. He started to get to his feet. A stabbing pain in his chest made him blow out his cheeks.

'Ow!'

The stabbing pain was now a dull ache, gnawing away inside his ribcage.

'What's the matter?'

'Are you sure the electrical equipment's safe?' Jon asked, clutching his shirt. 'It's done something to me.'

His father helped him over to a chair.

'Where does it hurt?'

'Well, my face is still burning from that stupid mask,' said Jon, remembering how it had clung to his skin. 'But it's my chest mostly.'

'Where?'

'About here.'

Jon touched his chest and winced.

'Jon,' said Dad, 'I think I can see a spot of blood.'

'Ow. I wouldn't be surprised. It really does hurt. This shouldn't happen, should it? I mean, I feel like I've been kicked by a horse.'

'I think we'd better take a look. Just unbutton your shirt.'

Jon did as he was told. As he gingerly unfastened the last button and pulled open his shirt, he heard his father gasp.

'What is it?'

He looked down. Covering the entire middle of his chest was a band of ugly, blue-black bruising, and right over his heart there was an ugly weal.

'This is impossible,' his father said.

35

Jon ran a finger gingerly over the raised ridge of flesh.

'I don't believe it.'

But it was true. The skin was actually broken.

'It's as if I really was shot by an arrow.'

4

The following afternoon Phoenix heard footsteps behind him.

'Hey, hold up.'

'I thought you had netball practice.'

'Cancelled.'

'Weird, isn't it?' said Phoenix. 'In a few days they're going to start selling a game that's about as safe as enriched plutonium, and here we are talking about netball practice. I wonder what we'll be doing come the end of the world, playing snakes and ladders?'

Laura gave him a sideways look.

'Life goes on,' she said. 'Until we find out who's developing the next part.'

'So you're ready to play again?'

'Try to stop me.'

'Good. I'd be lost without you.'

Laura was looking at Phoenix, wondering quite what to say next, when a red, single-decker bus swept past.

'Oh no!' she groaned. 'That's ours.'

'Forget it,' said Phoenix. 'It'll only take us twenty minutes to get home. Besides, I wouldn't mind a walk. Blow out the cobwebs.'

As they set off down the road, Laura nudged him. He seemed distracted.

'Some cobwebs. You're miles away.'

Phoenix chewed at the high collar of his coat.

'There's something else, isn't there? Go on, you can tell me.'

'It's Grandpa, he's dying.'

'But that's been going on for months. You already knew how ill he was.'

'No, I mean really dying. Mum got a phone call last night. They don't think he'll last the week.'

Laura squeezed his arm.

'I'm so sorry.'

Grandpa's death would see the snapping of a connection to the past, to Greece, to his twin brother, Andreas. The man who walked with Phoenix in his dreams.

Andreas.

'I wish I could have talked to Grandpa about Andreas. Really talk, I mean. Thirty years apart, Andreas and I each became aware of the myth-worlds. Maybe Grandpa could have helped me understand. Now there's no chance.'

'So what's happening?'

'Mum's going down to London tomorrow. We'll probably follow her at the weekend.'

'But what if somebody gets in touch about the game?'

'Not much I can do. He's my grandfather.'

Laura squeezed his arm again.

'I could look in on the house for you. Check your e-mails. I did it when you were away in Greece that time.'

'Do you want to come back now?' asked Phoenix. 'We'll ask Mum and Dad.'

Laura stopped and unzipped her bag.

'Hang on a minute. I'll phone Mum.'

She rummaged around inside.

'Where's that stupid mobile?'

While Laura was speaking to her mother, Phoenix watched the wind in the trees. He thought of Grandpa dying, and of Andreas, his twin brother who had died thirty years earlier, locked away in a madhouse. The first man to see the demons.

And the first to pay the price.

Half an hour later, in Phoenix's room, Laura interrupted his daydreams.

'A penny for your thoughts,' she said.

'Just thinking about Grandpa,' said Phoenix, 'and Andreas.'

'Imagine dying the way he did,' said Laura. 'Completely alone. A sane man shut up in an asylum.'

Phoenix didn't answer. He was staring intently at the carpet, remembering the story. How his great-uncle Andreas had been plagued by waking nightmares and been locked away for it. Those nightmares had come back to life in a computer game called *The Legendeer*. It was as if Andreas was actually there, in the room with them, prompting him, telling him where to look to unravel the mystery. Words came to him, like a spell, an incantation.

Everything lies veiled in numbers.

He saw them in his mind's eye. The sequences of threes, sixes and nines that filled the monitor screen and were printed on the gateway of light that opened to admit you deeper into the game.

'Right now somebody else is playing *The Legendeer*,' he said.

The words came again.

Everything lies veiled in numbers.

'But how do we find them, Laura? How do we warn them?'

5

Maybe Phoenix wouldn't have to warn anybody. Jon Jonsson had had his warning. It had taken three stitches at the hospital to close the wound.

'But how could this happen?' his mother demanded in the car on the way home.

'I've no idea,' Dad replied. 'I've examined the suit, gone over it with a fine-tooth comb in fact. There is nothing sharp in it, nothing that could inflict an injury like that. I don't understand it at all.'

'But what else could have caused it?'

'Nothing. I was standing right there beside him when it happened. He didn't hit anything. It's like he was struck by an invisible fist. It's a complete mystery.'

'Well, he's not playing it again,' Mum said firmly.

'I don't want to,' said Jon. 'It's evil.'

His mother looked round.

'What an odd thing to say. Don't you mean dangerous?'

No, he meant *evil*. Evil the way the Minotaur was evil. Evil the way Medusa was evil. Evil the way the vampyrs were evil. Evil. That's what held *The Legendeer* together.

'Evil, Mum, I mean evil.'

'Jon, you're worrying me.'

'You don't know what happened to me in that game. You can't even begin to imagine.'

His parents exchanged glances.

'I hope you're not going to take this lying down,' said his mother. 'This is our son's safety we're talking about. And he's completely terrified. What's that company of yours done to him?'

Jon sensed his father's irritation.

'It's not *my* company. I agreed to work for them in good faith. I didn't expect anything like this.'

Mum looked away.

'I'm sorry. I didn't mean to raise my voice. Look, don't you think I'm concerned? I've e-mailed Magna-com demanding an immediate explanation.'

'Why didn't you phone them? I'd want to speak to somebody in person about something this serious. For goodness' sake, it goes on sale in a few days.'

Jon watched his father shifting uneasily in the driving seat.

'I don't have a phone number.'

'I beg your pardon?'

'No telephone number. It was one of their rules from the very beginning, communication by e-mail only.'

'Are you telling me a major company like Magna-com doesn't even have a switchboard?'

'That's exactly what I'm saying. My salary is paid by computer and all messages come the same way. Come to think of it, I haven't dealt with a single flesh-and-blood human being once since I took the job.'

'What about at the interview?' Jon asked, suddenly more than interested. 'You must have met somebody then. Who took you on?'

'No interview,' Dad replied. 'I sent a cv by e-mail. Everything has been done by computer. I was impressed at first, the technology of the future and all that, but on second thoughts it does seem a bit odd.'

'A bit!' exclaimed Mum. 'I'd say it was downright sinister.'

41

They pulled up at the side of the house and stepped out onto the pavement, sprinkled with a fresh dusting of snow.

The discussion continued indoors.

'So you've never met a single person from Magna-com?'

'Never.'

'And never spoken to any of their people face to face?'

'Never.'

'I do wish you'd told me. Didn't it seem a bit strange?'

Jon soon tired of the argument. It wasn't getting anywhere. Leaving his parents to it, he headed for his room. Dad's workroom was now securely locked. Jon wouldn't be able to play *Warriors of the Raven* even if he wanted to. He undid a shirt button and touched his bandage gingerly. And he certainly didn't want to play, not if this was what it did to you. Buttoning up his shirt, he sat on his bed.

This is crazy.

Impossible.

But it had happened. He had the proof right there on his body.

'I've been wounded by a virtual arrow.'

It sounded even crazier said out loud. But the thump as it struck him, the stabbing pain through his heart, the hatred in Loki's yellow eyes, they were too real to be a mere game.

'What have we got ourselves into?'

He switched on his tv and channel-surfed for a few moments. He happened on a commercial for *Warriors of the Raven*. He watched it to the end then sat, hands on knees, facing his own PC.

There were no PR suits in his room and no disc for *Warriors of the Raven*. No danger, in other words. Yet he couldn't take his eyes off the screen.

I'm becoming completely paranoid.

But it wasn't paranoia. A game called *The Legendeer* had

brought fear into his predictable, cosy life. He thought about what Mum had said.

You're not going to take this lying down.

'So let's see what I can find out about you,' he said.

He sat down and typed in his password: *JJ*. He waited for a few moments for the Internet to connect then typed in the address of his favourite website.

www.ask arthur.com

He used it for his homework. You just typed in your question and it came up with a list of websites where you could get the information.

'Question: where do I find out about *The Legendeer*?'

Then he waited. He was offered twenty sites in all. *Legends of the world, Greek and Roman legends, Norse mythology.*

Then he saw what he was looking for.

www.legendeer.co.uk

He leaned forward and inspected the graphics on the opening page. The Minotaur, Medusa, werewolves, vampires, the images from the first two games.

'So what am I looking at, an unofficial fanzine?'

He scrolled down and started reading.

Have you played yet? Felt the Minotaur's breath on your neck? Heard the hiss of Medusa, the Vampyr's shriek?

That's exactly what it was, an electronic fanzine.

'Yeah, yeah,' he said. 'Been there, done that.'

Hooked on The Legendeer, Parts One and Two? the computer asked. **Can't wait to play the next one?**

'I've played it,' Jon said out loud. 'And I wish I hadn't.'

Counting the hours until it's out? The big one that Magna-com has been promising, the one with the Parallel Reality suits. Can you imagine it? Being transported body and soul into an alien world. Where you can see, hear, touch, even smell and taste your surroundings.

Now Jon *was* interested. The website had captured his

43

unsettling experience perfectly. But as he progressed through the questions, enthusiasm was replaced by something else. His blood ran cold. Excitement turned to horror. Suddenly every question seemed to be directed at him personally.

Have you looked into the face of terror, been impaled on eyes of pure evil? Said to yourself: this is real, this is real, this is real.

Too real.

His pulse quickened. But it was the final question that set it racing and made the back of his neck prickle.

Have you wondered about the mystery of the numbers, been drawn into their patterns, the power of three, the magic of nine, the trinity of trinities?

He remembered the snowstorm of numbers that came up every time Dad worked on *Warriors of the Raven*. They had wondered about them often.

The numbers. Yes, of course I've seen them.

Then the screen glowed with an elaborate pattern.

Threes . . .

. . . sixes . . .

. . . nines.

'That's right, that's what comes up.'

Have you noticed the connection between the world's mythologies? How so many things come in multiples of three? Whether it is ancient Greece or the Viking north, the pattern is the same. The nine rivers of Hades, the nine worlds of the Norse myths, the three Muses, the three Furies, the three Norns.

'Three Norns,' murmured Jon.

What about three-headed Cerberus, the three Gorgons, the three years of Fimbulwinter, the three rocks on which Loki's body is bound? The connections go on and on. That's what holds it all together. You have to understand— the myth-code rests on a base of three.

Jon pushed back the chair and stood up. Three Norns, three

rocks. He didn't know about the other stuff, but that certainly rang a bell.

'You do know something. Who are you? How could you . . . ?'

There was one final item at the bottom of the last page, an e-mail address.

Do you recognize the things we have mentioned? Have you been there? Have you been tempted by the golden portal of light, the gateway between the worlds? Want to share the experience with somebody? Then contact us.

Jon stared at the words, wondering whether he should trust them:

Contact us.

6

The phone call came on Friday night. Phoenix took it. Mum was in tears at the other end of the line.

'Phoenix, it's me. It's happened.'

'You mean he's . . . ?'

'Your grandfather passed away this afternoon.'

'I'm sorry, Mum.'

'At least his suffering is over. Put your dad on, will you?'

'Dad,' he called. 'You'd better take this. Mum's calling from London.'

'Coming.'

Dad mouthed a question:

Grandpa?

Phoenix nodded and stepped back. Grandpa dead. As he retreated to the study doorway, Phoenix saw the computer screen and felt a pang of anxiety. The funeral. They would be going down to London sometime soon. He would have to let Laura know. Just in case.

'Stupid,' he murmured. 'Nobody's been in touch for weeks. Why should it change now?'

But nothing would make the nagging doubt go away. However the odds were stacked against it, he couldn't quite accept that the game was over. He had an unfulfilled destiny. It had begun with Andreas and lived again through him. There was a chance, always a chance.

Dad hung up and turned round.

'The funeral is on Thursday. You'll have to take the day off school.'

As Phoenix made his way upstairs, he was acutely aware of the secret menace that had stolen into his life through the circuitry of the computer. Time was ticking away towards the deadline.

The launch of the game was approaching fast, and with it the unleashing of the demon threat. He hesitated at the top of the stairs. Hearing Dad behind him, he glanced back.

'Thinking about the game?'

Phoenix nodded.

'Aren't you?'

'I can't get it out of my mind,' said Dad. 'You know what comes out loud and clear from my reading of the Norse myths, what makes them stand out? It's this: Evil is predestined to win. That's what makes the Viking legends so different. The gods are so vulnerable, almost like ordinary men and women. Thor, Balder and the rest, they can all die and the forces of darkness can win. Even Odin, the king of the gods, loses an eye. The Gamesmaster couldn't have picked a better battle-ground than the Norse myths. In a world where Evil has the upper hand, the odds will be stacked against us.'

Phoenix stared at Dad. It all made sense. The Gamesmaster had chosen well. A land where Evil deals the cards.

'Anyway,' said Dad, 'I'm taking a shower.'

Phoenix watched Dad walking away along the landing. He had read the same books and now he was coming to the same conclusion. That's why the Gamesmaster had chosen the Viking world. It was to be the final victory of Evil.

Five minutes later, on his way back from the bathroom, Dad found Phoenix sitting on the bed.

'What's that you're reading?'

'Andreas' journal.'

'It's a wonder you don't know it off by heart by now.'

47

'I keep thinking that I'll find something in it,' said Phoenix.

Dad glanced at Phoenix sideways.

'There has to be something more we can do, something we've forgotten.'

'If there is, then I can't think of it.'

Phoenix rose to his feet.

'There has to be something *I* can do. Remember when Laura and I came back the last time, *I* did that.'

He remembered the second game, the final fight in the Vampyr's crypt. He had conjured the numbers. Not the computer, *him*. He remembered the way his fingers had prickled with a raw, elemental force. In a way, *he* had become the computer.

'It wasn't technology that brought us back. It was . . . a power. The same power Andreas felt when he saw *his* demons. I've inherited it from him, I just know it. I can't explain it, but it's got something to do with the numbers. I could read them. I made the gateway open.'

He couldn't work out Dad's expression. Was he really interested or was he just humouring him?

'Go on.'

'The question is: why can't I do it again? Why can't I find my way to wherever the Gamesmaster is?'

'I don't know,' said Dad. 'Have you tried?'

'Have I tried! I've done nothing but try. I just can't call up the numbers in the right order. I have a theory.'

He didn't tell Dad how it had come to him, the night before. In a dream, of course.

'You want to hear it?'

'Fire away.'

'There's a different sequence to each of the myth-worlds. It's like the combination to a safe. Get the combination right and the tumblers fall into place. Open sesame, you're entering a different world.'

'But you can't get the right combination?'

Phoenix raised his eyebrows.

'Can you imagine just how many permutations of three, six and nine there can be? I don't even know how many numbers there are in the sequence. There could be three. There could be ten. There could be thirty. It's harder than winning the National Lottery!'

Dad set off down the landing.

'The Gamesmaster won't win,' he said. 'We will stop him, you know.'

Phoenix followed.

'How?'

He caught up with Dad and looked him in the eye.

'There's just over a week left before *Warriors of the Raven* comes out. We're going to stop him, are we? Go on, tell me how?'

Dad wished he'd kept quiet. Finally he was forced to admit:

'I don't know.'

7

If Jon Jonsson brought up the *Legendeer* website once in the next few days, he must have done it a hundred times. He was like a non-swimmer diving in at the deep end. He stood all ready to go, trembling with anticipation, but he could never quite bring himself to take the plunge.

'I just wish I knew what to do.'

Dad was no use. He'd been dithering too. Stay with Magnacom, or just make a clean break and resign? He had sent his e-mails, loads of them. He had demanded a meeting with the company, but all that had come back was a message thanking him for his work on the game, and a fat cheque by way of a bonus.

'It's a bribe,' Dad had said when he opened the envelope. 'They want me to keep my mouth shut.'

Other than that there was nothing. No apology, no explanation for the accident, no hint that they were taking him seriously. But instead of coming to a decision, he would just wander outside and smash at the outhouse with his hammer. As if he were smashing away at an unknown enemy. Jon shut his computer down and wandered downstairs. Mum was at her evening class. As for Dad, no prizes for guessing where he would be.

'Dad, are you in the workroom?'

'Yes. Do you need me?'

Jon hovered in the doorway. He hadn't entered the room since playing the game the second time.

'No, I just wondered what you were going to do?'

Dad was packing the PR suit in a cardboard box.

'I've made my mind up. Magna-com have fobbed me off long enough. They're taking me for an idiot. This is their last chance. I've been in touch with that consumer programme on the television, the one your mother likes. If I don't get a satisfactory explanation from the company, I'm going to send them the game and all the equipment. There is something seriously wrong with it. It can't go on sale, not like this.'

He taped up the box, addressed a sticky label and pressed it down.

'I've e-mailed Magna-com, telling them what I intend to do. I'm giving them a few days to provide me with a proper explanation, then all this goes to the reporter I've been speaking to.'

'Wow, you have thought it through, haven't you?'

Dad smiled grimly.

'Jon, what happened to you was really serious. I can't have any other youngsters hurt by this company's negligence.'

Dad joined Jon in the hallway and locked the workroom door from outside.

'That's where the game and the PR suits are going to stay until I hear from Magna-com, or until I am forced to go to the media.'

Jon nodded. Dad had finally made his mind up.

Fair enough. Now I'm going to do the same.

He went back to his room and typed in the website address:
www.legendeer.co.uk

He scrolled down and copied the e-mail address.

'Let's see what you've got to say for yourselves.'

Phoenix wasn't part of Grandpa's funeral. He was there, but he didn't want to talk to anyone. His mind was elsewhere, with the twin brother nobody mentioned.

51

He hovered at the edge of the funeral party and watched Great-aunt Sophia. She must have been remembering Andreas too at that moment, almost as much as she was remembering Grandpa, but she didn't mention him. Not once the whole day. He remained a kind of ghost, a darkness at the edge of the family's lives. He drifted over to the sideboard and looked at the collection of family photographs. No Andreas.

'I know what you're thinking.'

Phoenix turned round.

'Aunt Sophia.'

'We did Andreas a terrible wrong.'

It was a shock to hear her even mention him. Phoenix was about to mumble a reply, but she held up her hand.

'No, you don't need to be polite. You don't need to forgive. I am an old woman. I can do without such pleasantries. We let the villagers get away with a terrible crime. All because they closed their eyes to the nightmare world. Andreas was telling the truth. There is horror all around us. There *is* a nightmare world.'

'Then you know Andreas wasn't crazy?'

'Of course. I always knew, but I was afraid, afraid to be different like Andreas. I didn't have his courage. I didn't dare walk alone.'

There was a moment's silence, then she spoke in a hushed voice.

'It's happening again, isn't it? Your mother told me.'

Phoenix returned her stare.

'Yes, it's happening again.'

'Then you must not be afraid as we were. You must face the darkness. You must fulfil my brother's destiny.'

And that was it. Pressing a small, black and white photograph into Phoenix's hand, she walked away. Phoenix examined it, a photo of the brothers standing in front of a whitewashed house in Greece. He wondered exactly how, with just two days left before the game's launch, he could fulfil his destiny, when his mobile phone rang.

'Phoenix, it's come.'

'Laura?'

'I've just checked your computer. You've got an e-mail from Iceland.'

'Iceland! Why Iceland?'

'It's a boy called Jon. His father is the one. He's been working on *Warriors of the Raven* and it's all going wrong. Phoenix, it's just like you and your dad all over again. I've already e-mailed Jon back. He can send us a copy of the game, Phoenix. It's the breakthrough we've been looking for.'

Phoenix looked down at Andreas' face and smiled. So Dad was right. They had moved it abroad.

'Thanks, Laura. I'll tell Dad. We'll be home tonight.'

8

Jon's parents were still at work when he got home from school. He glanced at the hallway clock. They should be home any time. Just a few minutes until he told Dad about the website. He took the latest e-mail from his pocket. The print-out was tattered with repeated reading. He almost knew it off by heart. It didn't prevent him reading it again:

Jon,

You're right. There is something wrong with the game. What you saw wasn't just graphics. It's a real world. That's right, every bit as real as this one. I have been there. I've been in the position you are now, but I went through the gateway and became part of its world. The first two games were just like the one you entered, but we got in the way of the Gamesmaster's plans. What Magnacom put on the market was just a pale imitation of the real thing. Now it's starting all over again. Through this game the barrier between the worlds can be broken down. We can enter the nightmare world of the ancient myths. And the creatures from that world can break into ours. Do you understand what I'm telling you? Monsters could walk among us.

That's what your father has been paid to do. He wasn't helping to write a computer game. He was bringing the two worlds into line. He was making it possible for the demons you have seen to break through. Imagine what that would be like. Your worst imaginings come true. And it's tomorrow, Jon.

Tomorrow!

But it isn't too late. There is something you must do. Send me the game, or at least a copy. It is the only way I can stop the nightmare from happening.

If you have been inside the game, you know what I'm talking about.

Send it, Jon. Send me the game.

Phoenix.

Jon looked at the locked workroom door. The sealed package was inside. For a moment he actually thought about smashing his way in. But he rejected the idea just as quickly.

I'll get the game to you.

But how do I convince Dad?

He knew that what Phoenix had told him was true. Anyone who had entered the world of the game would be convinced. But would Dad be so sure? Jon returned to the living room and drew back the blinds to look up the road for his father. Just as he was moving away from the window, he caught a glimpse of something. It flickered across his field of vision, sending a shudder through him. But there was no doubt about it. Somebody was inside the house with him.

'Who's there?' he asked.

There was no reply, but he hadn't been imagining things. There was definitely a noise, and it was coming from the workroom.

But how?

It was locked.

'Mum, Dad, is that you?'

But he knew it wasn't them. Jon edged to the door, peering up the hallway. His heart missed a beat. Whoever was moving around the flat had left a trail of paper clips on the floor. It was no accident, either. It was a deliberate act, meant to unnerve him. The intruder was putting on a show. The trail of clips was to let him know he wasn't alone. The plastic pot that had held them was still rocking outside the kitchen.

55

Worse still, the intruder was between Jon and escape. Panic took hold, coiling round his windpipe, choking off his breath.

Got to think.

But he couldn't think. He looked around the room for something to defend himself, but immediately snapped back to attention. The empty pot had changed direction and was starting to roll towards him. It hadn't shifted by itself. Somebody was making it roll.

'Who are you?' he called, his voice sounding feebler and fainter than ever.

Discovering a burglar had always been one of his worst fears. Now he would have given anything for it to be a burglar. He remembered what it said on tv. If you disturb someone breaking and entering they usually run. But this intruder wasn't running.

'Who's there?'

There was no reply, just another pot rolling into the hallway. Then another and another. Six plastic pots in all, spilling pencils, erasers, drawing pins. The intruder was teasing, mischievous.

'Please stop it,' Jon said.

Immediately, he regretted saying it. That's what the intruder wanted, to have him begging and pleading. That's what the pots were all about. Cat and mouse. A power game. He wasn't doing it because he had to. He was doing it because *he liked it*.

Belatedly, Jon changed tack:

'I'm not afraid of you.'

Even that was counterproductive.

The intruder spoke for the first time, in a sing-song voice tinged with malice.

'Poor little Jon, all alone. Not afraid, you say?'

He stepped out into the corridor. Jon gasped.

'Then you should be.'

It was *him*, the owner of the yellow eyes.

'Please don't hurt me.'

Jon was trying to make sense of the evidence of his eyes. Facing him was a puzzle rather than a human being. He had the face of a teenage boy, but the muscular frame of a grown man. Then there were those eyes, Loki's eyes.

'Oh, I'm not going to hurt you,' the intruder told him. 'Not that I couldn't if I felt like it. There's no need. I just came to get this.'

He was holding up the computer equipment from the study, the *Warriors of the Raven* disc, a PR suit and a points bracelet.

Jon shook his head.

'You can't have it. It doesn't belong to you.'

The intruder took a step forward, a look of bored amusement on his face.

'And who is going to take it from me? You?'

He shoved the PR suit and points bracelet back in their box.

'Your father had a job to do. He shouldn't have interfered.'

Jon thought of Phoenix waiting for the disc.

It's the only way to stop the nightmare.

'You've got to give them back.'

'I don't *have* to do anything. That's the beauty of serving the Gamesmaster. It gives you total freedom.'

The intruder smiled.

'How can I explain it to you? How can I make you understand how stupid it is for you to give me orders? The Gamesmaster isn't a man, you see. He is a power. For many years he has been a power trapped in another world, a ghost, a phantom. Now he is about to rise. He is a power that will make the worlds tremble. And I serve that power. I am its hands and eyes. Now do you see why you shouldn't tell me what to do?'

Jon was wondering what to say when he heard a key scraping in the lock.

'Dad.'

'Well, fun over,' said the intruder, picking up the box. 'I've got what I came for. Time for me to go.'

He walked straight past Jon and into the workroom. Jon followed him with his eyes, then turned to greet his father.

'Jon, who were you talking to? Who's in there with **you?**'

Not knowing what to say, Jon gave the only answer he could.

'Somebody is in the workroom. He's got all the game gear.'

Dad pushed past him and stared for a moment at the splintered doorframe, the broken lock. It had clearly been smashed open from the inside.

'What the . . . ?'

He walked into the workroom.

'Dad, be careful.'

But Dad turned round.

'Jon, there's nobody here.'

9

Phoenix and Laura sat side by side at the computer. John Graves stood behind them, looking over their shoulders. The e-mail from Jon Jonsson made grim reading.

Phoenix,

I've let you down. I know this sounds crazy, but it was him. Loki. We've been robbed by a character in a computer game! There really is no other explanation. The workroom window was locked. He came out of the PC and took everything. I've blown it.

Jon.

'He's got the game!' Laura exclaimed. 'Now what do we do?'

Phoenix closed his eyes.

'Give me a moment to think.'

'But without the game, we can't follow Adams. We can't do anything. It was Adams, wasn't it?'

'Oh, it was him all right. He's the only one of the Gamesmaster's disciples who can pass through the gateway. From what Jon tells us, he's obviously taken the part of Loki in the game. The Mischief-Maker, most cunning and evil of the Norse gods. Suits him, don't you think?'

Phoenix fingered the photo of Andreas and stared at the screen.

'Well?'

'I'm still thinking.'

He lowered his head, as if turning in on himself. After a few moments he looked up.

'I have to play in Jon's place. I'm the only one who can end this nightmare. I'm the Legendeer. I've got to go in after Adams, take the part of Heimdall, Loki's arch-enemy. I will be the hero.'

The screen-save clicked on, planets, stars and comets. Phoenix frowned.

'What is it?' Dad asked. 'Speak to us, Phoenix.'

'I wonder.'

'What? Tell us what you're thinking about.'

Phoenix stared at the screen-save for a few more moments, then brought up E-mail Express again. He clicked Compose Message.

'What are you doing?'

'Trying a long shot. Dad, do you remember what I told you? About the numbers, I mean?'

'That they're the language of the game and you think you can manipulate them? Of course I remember.'

'Now's the time to test my theory,' said Phoenix.

Fulfil Andreas' destiny, Great-aunt Sophia had told him. Maybe he still could. He typed in his message:

Jon,

You've no need to feel guilty. There's nothing you could do. The person you saw is called Steve Adams. He entered the game about the same time I did, but when it came to taking sides, he chose darkness. He does the dirty work for the one who controls the game, the Gamesmaster. You recognized him because he plays a part in it. We play the hero, he plays the villain. That's right, in a way it *was* Loki you saw in your flat. Now think. We've got one chance left. The game works on a computer language, something completely different to most information technology. The base number is three. Do those numbers appear on your father's PC? Does it mean anything to you? You have to look for them. I repeat: multiples of three.

This is urgent.

Phoenix.

He hit Send and drummed his fingers impatiently on the computer table.

'This is crazy,' said Dad. 'We're relying on a fourteen-year-old boy.'

'Dad,' Phoenix said coolly, '*I'm* a fourteen-year-old boy.'

The reply came a few moments later:

Phoenix,

Yes, I've seen the numbers you mean. They're flashing on the screen right now. What do you want me to do?

Jon

Phoenix looked at Dad and Laura, then wrote a new message:

Jon,

You've got to act immediately.

Go to the computer and look for any strings of numbers you can recognize. I know it's hard. You will see hundreds of numbers, maybe thousands, but they are not random. There *are* patterns. You've got to look for clear combinations. Hurry. Our enemy could be reading this message.

Phoenix.

Laura read the e-mail. As Phoenix hit Send, she asked him the obvious question:

'Will this work?'

Phoenix glanced over his shoulder, as if for support. Dad shrugged his shoulders:

'You're the Legendeer, son. You tell us.'

'I've no idea, but I've got to try.'

10

Jon glanced out of the window. Mum and Dad were standing on the pavement, talking to the policeman. He had come to take a statement while Jon was exchanging e-mails with Phoenix. For a frustrating quarter of an hour, while his mind raced with thoughts of magic numbers and other worlds, Jon had had to tell his story over and over again. He had wisely omitted any mention of the intruder being a character out of a computer game. Finally, the policeman had enough information and Jon could run to the computer. It was still blinking away, the way it had been when the intruder came.

Jon sat down in front of the monitor screen and there they were, the confusion of numbers.

The language of the game.

The language of other worlds.

*There **is** a way.*

He gave another quick glance out of the window. His parents were still talking to the policeman.

'A sequence,' he murmured. 'Look for a sequence.'

It was easier said than done. What confronted him was a snowstorm of seemingly unrelated numerals.

'This is hopeless.'

He remembered the optical illusions some of his friends had brought into school and the advice that helped you find the hidden picture.

*Fix your attention on one spot and look **through** the pattern.*

It was easier said than done.

'Oh, come on, Jon, you can do it. Now focus.'

Then, suddenly, amid what had appeared an impenetrable maze of numbers, he was able to make out a sequence.

For a moment he couldn't believe his eyes, but there it was.

3–3–3 3–6–9 3–3–3

A definite string of numerals. It seemed to detach itself, take on solid form and present itself to him, a single distinct combination. He scribbled down the numbers and stood up.

'Got it.'

That's when it happened. The screen began to clear. In place of the numbers there was a fiery background, and in place of the sequence was a familiar face. The hard, cheerless features. The yellow, hateful eyes.

'You!'

'Surprise surprise.'

Then a golden light was filling the room. Jon retreated to the door. The numerals that had so recently been racing on the monitor screen were pulsating in the portal of light.

It's the gateway.

He's coming through.

Thinking quickly, Jon yanked the plug from the wall.

'No power, no entry,' he said.

To his horror, it made no difference. The PC continued to purr, powered by something stronger than electricity. The gateway continued to shimmer. The intruder was coming back. It was him, Adams.

'The numbers. Of course, you want the numbers.'

Jon turned and ran to his room where his own PC was on, the prepared e-mail ready to go. All it needed was the numbers. Jon started typing:

3–3–3

'I wouldn't do that.'

The back of Jon's neck prickled.

Adams was in the doorway. He was standing right behind him.

3–6–9

Jon felt strong fingers closing round his arms.

'I said: I wouldn't do that.'

Before Jon could struggle or protest, he was flung bodily across the room. He picked himself up to see Adams leaning over the keyboard.

'No, get away from it.'

Just as the words were leaving Jon's lips, the front door slammed.

'Dad, Mum, up here!'

Adams turned.

'You'll regret you ever said that.'

Dad was already on the landing outside the room.

'Jon, what's wrong?'

Then Dad saw Adams and the blood drained from his face.

'Where did you come from? Get away from my son.'

He threw himself at Adams, propelling him against the wall. It was a brief struggle. Adams possessed the power of the myth-world. He easily shrugged Dad off and sent him crashing into the doorframe. But it gave Jon the time he needed. He scrambled to the keyboard and typed in the last three digits:

3–3–3

As Adams turned and saw what he had done, Jon smiled triumphantly and guided the mouse across the pad.

'You won't win,' he shouted defiantly.

For the first time, the superior sneer vanished from Adams' face.

Delighted at the reaction, Jon left-clicked the mouse to dispatch the e-mail.

Send.

11

'You know what I've got to do, don't you? If Jon finds the numbers, I mean.'

'Yes,' said Dad. 'We've been here before, remember. Your mother and I both understand. You're the Legendeer. You have to fulfil your destiny.'

He tapped the monitor screen.

'We'll be watching your every move, just like the other times.'

Phoenix smiled grimly.

'*If* we get the numbers.'

Then, as the words left his lips, a single digit registered in the Inbox:

(1)

'Open it,' Dad said excitedly.

It was exactly what they'd been waiting for:

3–3–3 3–6–9 3–3–3

Phoenix scribbled down the numbers, then looked at Laura.

'There's no time to lose.'

She nodded.

He turned to his father.

'It's all right, Phoenix,' he said. 'There's nothing more to say. Finish it.'

Phoenix smiled and reread the string of numerals. He picked up a points bracelet and snapped it onto his wrist. Then he did what he had done in the Vampyr's crypt. He started to trace the numbers, sketching them in the air with his finger.

If I really am the Legendeer, this is going to work.

He traced the numbers again:

3–3–3 3–6–9 3–3–3

It was an electronic Open Sesame.

Within moments the screen had begun to clear. There in front of his eyes was a wintry landscape. Amid a howling blizzard he could make out a rocky outcrop, and beyond that he could just about distinguish seven bands of glittering colour.

'Bifrost,' he said, recognizing it from his reading of the Norse myths. 'The rainbow bridge.'

Phoenix laid his hands flat on the screen, as if reaching out to it, and a magical transformation occurred. It became liquid, malleable to the touch. He was able to prise it open, just like molten plastic. He was tearing a hole in reality.

I can do it.

I really can!

'Dad,' he cried, thrilled by what he had done. 'Dad!'

But the transformation was accelerating. A shimmering golden oval had appeared, imprinted with silver numbers, the combination he had traced on the monitor screen. Phoenix held out his hand to Laura, and she took it.

'There's no going back,' he said.

'Good,' she replied. 'Because I don't want to go back.'

They both turned and waved to John Graves, but he was already a barely distinct, blurred figure. Phoenix and Laura stepped into the portal of light, passing through the gateway and closing the door to their old world behind them.

BOOK TWO

—

The Book of the Gamesmaster

THE LEVELS

———

Level Nine
Warriors of the Raven

1

Phoenix was spiralling through time and place, spinning and tumbling out of control, and when the spinning stopped he found himself lying sprawled on a blanket of snow. What confronted him on the other side of the gateway was a high-ridged landscape whipped by bitter north-easterly winds. For a moment, flashing against the grey sky he saw a menu, as if lit in neon. Only one option was highlighted:

Level 9. Warriors of the Raven.

As the flashing menu faded, Phoenix turned away. His thoughts were directed at the Gamesmaster:

Still going through the motions, are you?

Still pretending it's all a game.

But everything around him reminded Phoenix that this was much more than that. He was standing on a bare hillside, some hundred metres from the summit of a claw-shaped crag, overlooking the waters of a frozen inlet. Half a dozen longships were beached on the shore. The peak was awhirl with a furious blizzard and the bitter cold sank its teeth right into the marrow of his bones. He knew that back in Dad's study there was no Phoenix and no Laura. They had entered another world entirely.

I'm back.

He looked around for Laura.

'Where is she?' he wondered, peering into the storm.

Then he noticed something. Half-lost in the swirling mass of flakes there was a building. What was it, a stone cairn, a derelict chapel?

'Laura, are you in there?'

He continued up the hill in silence and stopped at the wall of the stone pile before them.

'What is this place?' he murmured, inspecting the carved symbols that covered the stonework.

The wind was howling and whipping against his face as if trying to cast him out.

'Laura?'

He was about to make his way inside the mysterious structure, when he heard her voice.

'Laura?' he asked.

'In here.'

There were more carvings inside, grotesque images of giants and elves, witches and dragons.

'What is all this?' she asked.

'This,' said Phoenix, touching the roughly scored lettering beneath the pictures, 'is the runic alphabet. The Vikings carved these letters on wood or stone. Each letter is meant to possess magic powers.'

'Can you read them?'

Phoenix shook his head.

'But look at this. The episodes are laid out in levels. I think this one's the death of Balder, the level Jon played in the game. This is where we are now, see the outline of the building and this . . .'

His voice trailed off. He had become aware of Laura staring at something behind him.

'What's wrong?'

Her dark eyes flicked in the direction of three hooded women. They seemed to have appeared from nowhere.

'You are welcome back, player,' they said. 'So you changed your mind? You wish to enter our world.'

'You mistake me for somebody else,' said Phoenix.

At the sound of his voice, the women appeared startled and confused. They huddled together, discussing the turn of events in hushed voices.

'We did not read this in the runes,' said one in a dismayed voice. 'This was not meant to be.'

'You must leave,' cried another. 'Your presence upsets the balance of the world. You cannot go against Fate.'

'Get away,' shrieked the third, waving Phoenix away. 'The runes forbid your presence.'

'Then consult them again,' he retorted. 'I'm not leaving.'

Once again the three women turned away, whispering and gesturing.

'We are the Norns,' they told him finally. 'Our power is as ancient as the stones. The fate of men is in our hands. Who are you to command us?'

'You know who I am,' said Phoenix. 'I am Heimdall.'

'No, you are not the one.'

'I am Heimdall,' Phoenix repeated in a strong, defiant voice. 'I belong here. Now do as I say. Consult the runes.'

'You crave your destiny,' said one of the Norns. 'And we have no power to deny you. You claim the name of Heimdall. So be it.'

'But know this,' said another. 'It is a dangerous hunger you have in your belly.'

The third detached herself from the others and rattled half a dozen stones in her bony hand before tossing them to the ground. Five lay on their faces. She crouched down and examined the single upturned stone. It was etched with a symbol.

'I am Verdande,' said the Norn, picking up the stone. 'I represent the past. This rune is called Mannaz. It stands for Man. You will champion the cause of Man.'

Phoenix nodded. 'Mankind is threatened. I am here to defend it.'

His words set off much muttering among the Norns. The second of the sisters stepped forward to throw the runes. Again just one lay face up.

'I am Urd. I represent the present. This rune is called Ansuz. It stands for Odin and the other gods of Asgard, the Aesir.'

'I am here to fight at the side of the Aesir against the forces of darkness.'

The Norns exchanged glances. The third of the Norns cast her runes.

'I am Skuld. I represent the future. This rune is called Raido, the rune of journeying. Your path will be long and dangerous. I see the shadow of death falling across it. Look about you – we've had three years of Fimbulwinter, heavy snow everywhere, no sign of blessed summer. Ill-doing surrounds us like a sour mist. The forces of darkness gather and life hangs by a slender thread. It is Heimdall's destiny to be a beacon in the darkness.'

72

Laura looked at Phoenix. He was unmoved.

'Tell me something I don't know. Now, we'd be grateful if you would set us on our way.'

The Norns gathered together whispering to each other. Finally they turned to face Phoenix and Laura.

'You have come this far, so we must guide you, but your destiny awaits you in this frozen Northland. It may not be the one you wished for. Great Odin gave one of his eyes to gain wisdom. It is a quality you would do well to prize. You have time to reconsider. You were not meant to come. The Northland rebels against your presence. You may still turn back.'

'There's no turning back,' said Phoenix. 'Show us the way.'

'The past you know,' said Verdande. 'Loki has used trickery to slay brave Balder. For his crime the Mischief-Maker is bound in chains at the end of the world. His blood beats with rage against the gods of Asgard.'

'So here you stand,' said Urd. 'Men will look upon you and know you a Heimdall, watchman of the gods. If you go on you will draw the ire of Loki and all his legions. Do you still want Heimdall's destiny?'

'If it's the part I have to play,' said Phoenix. 'Fine, I'm Heimdall.'

Urd scowled. She didn't appreciate his flippant answer.

'The future is yours to make,' said Skuld. 'The world shivers under endless winter. Men wait in vain for the coming of summer. The Age of Evil has come upon earth. The world is hard and cruel. Brothers slay brothers. Daughters betray mothers. The wicked fall upon the innocent and the good, while their protectors cower behind locked doors. Soon Loki will break his chains and lead them. On the fateful day of Ragnarok you must raise an army of men and gods. At Vigrid plain you must fight the Mischief-Maker and his legions. It will fall to you to meet yellow-eyed Loki in fearful battle. Do you still crave Heimdall's fate?'

'It's why I came,' said Phoenix.

'Then the die is cast,' said Skuld. 'Men will know you as Heimdall, watchman of Asgard. Fulfil your destiny.'

The wind roared, hail stung Phoenix and Laura's eyes. When they were able to look again, the Norns had gone.

2

'We still don't know which way to go,' said Laura, crossing the floor of the stone building. 'In fact they didn't tell us anything.'

Phoenix nodded.

'I don't think it matters. Something will show us the way.'

He awaited the secret speaker who had guided him before. He awaited the voice of Andreas.

'Or someone.'

Laura walked outside onto the misty hillside.

Phoenix was following her when she recoiled, bumping into him.

'What is it?'

She turned round. Her eyes were hard points of horror. Phoenix saw what had startled her. Hanging by a noose from a single, twisted oak tree was a corpse. It was turning slowly like a compass needle from north to east, then from east to south, the rope round its neck creaking under the weight. Phoenix stared. The corpse filled him with unease.

'Phoenix,' called Laura. 'Why don't you come away?'

'Something isn't right,' he told her.

Then he realized. One finger on its right hand was moving. Ever so slightly it's true, but there was definite movement.

It was alive.

A moment later two, no three, fingers were twitching compulsively. Then all five fingers were flexing. Before Phoenix knew it, the right arm was bending slowly at the elbow. He could see muscles and tendons moving through the rotting flesh. Then the creature was reaching up towards the rope.

The left arm followed suit and both hands started to grip the branch of the ancient oak. Hand over hand, the corpse began to haul itself up. There was immense power in its arms and they lifted the body until the rope went slack around its neck. With a couple of tugs followed by a macabre shrug of the shoulders, the head was free.

'I know this,' said Phoenix. 'This thing is a dead-walker. A man who dies as a hero in battle ascends to Valhalla. A man who dies any other way, like this one hanging from a noose, joins the unhappy dead and dwells with the queen of the Underworld, Hela. This is one of her creatures, a zombie.'

The creature dropped to earth and turned in their direction. Was this the kind of monster the Gamesmaster planned to release into his world?

'Laura,' Phoenix yelled. 'Run!'

'Run where?' cried Laura.

'Who cares?' Phoenix snapped, fleeing himself. 'Just run!'

They'd put fifty metres between themselves and the lonely building before Laura ventured her first glance back.

'Is it there?'

'Don't ask,' he panted. 'Don't talk. Don't even think.'

He was unarmed and unsure what he was dealing with.

'Just run.'

The creature was marching on, half-hidden by the swirling haze of snow.

'How do we stop that thing?' he said.

'Keep going,' cried Laura. 'There's something ahead, at the bottom of the hill.'

In the hollow there was another building, made of wood this time. A plume of smoke rose from a hole in the roof.

'Look, see the smoke? That means there are people in there.'

'I wish I knew exactly who was in there,' said Phoenix, hesitating.

'With that thing following us,' Laura panted, 'I think it's worth taking the chance. If they're sitting around a fire, at least they are flesh and blood.'

She forced the pace.

'Well, what do you say? Anything is better than our zombie friend.'

They were standing in front of the door of the building that was their destination. Phoenix reached for the finely wrought handle.

'Now *I'm* having second thoughts,' said Laura. 'I hope we're doing the right thing.'

Phoenix pulled open the door.

'I don't think we've got much choice.'

The moment he opened the door, Phoenix wondered whether Laura hadn't been right after all. They had stepped into a wild feast, a riotous affair lit by torches and a huge log fire. In a hall hung with rows of decorated shields, pelts and battle-axes, dozens of burly, bearded men were gathered around a long table. A huge banner emblazoned with a giant black bird hung over their heads.

'A raven,' hissed Phoenix. 'The symbol of Odin. Father of the gods.'

Laura accepted the information but looked around aghast.

'Phoenix, I think we've made a mistake.'

The diners were shouting and laughing, and noisily draining their ale from drinking horns. The air was heavy with wood-smoke and the spit and hiss of roasting meat. But the entry of the two teenagers brought everything to an abrupt halt.

'Ye gods,' said a great ox of a man as he rose from his seat. 'What have we here?'

He inspected Laura and Phoenix from head to toe.

'They're not Northmen,' barked a second man, his blue eyes cold with hostility. 'That's for sure.'

Phoenix and Laura edged closer together for support. They had their hands on the door jamb and were probably turning the same difficult decision over in their minds. Stay and face the rough justice of this rowdy, drunken gathering or flee and risk running into the dead-walker out in the storm. It was Phoenix who made the decision. Shoving the door closed behind him, he took a step forward.

'My name is . . .'

He'd chosen to put on a bold front, but it backfired. Before he could name himself as Heimdall, the man who had spoken first dashed his drinking horn down on the table.

'Who told you to speak, boy!'

Laura's fingers tightened on Phoenix's arm, her nails digging into him.

'No man – no, nor unshaven boy, either – enters the mead-hall of Halfdan Forkbeard uninvited and presumes to speak without my bidding.'

'I didn't . . .'

The man who had announced himself as Halfdan Forkbeard threw his arms wide and thundered out his words to the entire gathering.

'Will you listen to him? There he goes again. Have you ever heard the like of it? This pimply cub thinks he can just walk into the hall of the Berserkers and presume to speak. He needs to be taught a lesson.'

'Yes,' came a voice from the back of the hall. 'And you're the man to give it to him, Halfdan Forkbeard.'

The speaker was greeted with a roar of approval.

'Have you heard of me, lad?' demanded Halfdan, planting his fists on his hips. 'I am the sword-wielder, the wolf-wrestler and dragon-master. I march beneath the raven banner of the All-father. My ships have combed the bright sea-tresses from here to the edge of the poisoned sea. Do you know this name that makes the mountains shiver?'

Phoenix weighed up his options. In the end, he thought it better to say nothing.

'I am Halfdan Forkbeard, Jarl of Skaldheim, Lord of Berserkers. I am defender of the gods of Asgard, ring-giver of heroes, ice-strider, slayer of the dead-walkers and all demons of the night. Kneel, boy.'

Phoenix was all too ready to bow his head, if only under the weight of the chieftain's many titles. In fact, at that moment Phoenix would have readily flattened himself before Halfdan and kissed his boots. What stopped him was the silent speaker, a voice from far away that only he heard.

No, face this man.

Phoenix nodded grimly. There was certainty in the voice. He had to do as he was told. He had to act like an envoy of the gods. Phoenix gave Halfdan Forkbeard his answer in a quavering voice:

'I am afraid I can't kneel to you, Halfdan Forkbeard.'

His reply was met with a loud gasp.

Laura dug her nails into the back of his hand. This time she almost drew blood.

'What are you doing?'

'I'm not exactly sure.'

Halfdan strode forward until he was standing, feet planted apart, inches from Phoenix. Phoenix was tall and well-built for his fourteen years, but Halfdan easily eclipsed him both in height and bulk.

'By the beard of Odin,' roared the huge figure, his own grease-stiffened beard wagging menacingly. 'Do you know who you're speaking to? I've ground the skulls of men bigger than you, and picked my teeth with their bones.'

Phoenix heard the voice again.

Courage.

79

He had to make a show of boldness.

'I am speaking to Halfdan Forkbeard,' said Phoenix, barely able to stop his legs giving way beneath him. 'The man who *claims* to slay the dead-walkers.'

This time the hall was stunned to silence.

'But my companion and I have just encountered one of the undead.'

A murmur ran through the gathering.

'That's right,' said Phoenix, finding his voice. 'There it was, large as death, and within spitting distance of this hall. Not too scared of you, was it? Where were you when you were needed, Jarl of Skaldheim?'

Halfdan gestured to two of his warriors.

'Take a look outside.'

But Phoenix had become intoxicated by the danger of his words, and was letting his tongue run just a little too far:

'Hiding in your drinking horn, were you, Lord Halfdan?'

There were no gasps of astonishment this time. The entire crowd were leaning forward, their interest in the impudent stranger intense. What gave this sapling the gall to insult a great oak like Halfdan Forkbeard?

'Nothing,' Halfdan's men reported on their return, the blizzard's blast following them into the hall.

'What do you say to that, boy?' demanded Halfdan. 'I hope you have a good answer. Bloodletter here knows how to deal with those who cross me.'

He ran a finger down the edge of his battle-axe.

'I say,' Phoenix told him, 'that I am here on a mission to raise an army.'

'An army, eh?' chuckled Halfdan. 'And who sent you on this mission?'

'I do the will of the gods,' said Phoenix.

A murmur went round the hall.

'I am Heimdall, watchman of Asgard.'

The claim provoked outrage.

'Blasphemy,' cried some.

Halfdan held up his hand for silence.

'Heimdall, are you?' asked Halfdan. 'The far-seer, the watchman of the gods?'

'I am.'

'He's no god,' protested a warrior at the back. 'Send him back out into the storm, ring-giver.'

Halfdan strode around the hall, raising his arms.

'No, my brothers,' he said. 'We dare not risk the wrath of the gods.'

Halfdan eyed Phoenix warily.

'Odin, lord of Asgard,' he roared. 'Thor, the thunderer, I appeal to you. If this is indeed your watchman, send me a sign.'

His speech brought renewed protests and demands for Phoenix's head. Other voices counselled caution.

'Do it, Halfdan, call upon the gods.'

The quarrel looked like getting out of hand but the hubbub subsided as quickly as it had begun. There was a loud knock at the door. In the hushed silence that followed, fearful glances were exchanged.

'It can't be.'

The knock came again, so loud and forceful it almost smashed the door.

'Who will answer it?' asked Halfdan.

Nobody stirred.

'What's the matter, zombie-slayer?' asked Phoenix, his confidence growing. 'Afraid of who is on the other side of the door?'

Halfdan spun round, confusion written on his broad face.

'No, it's a trick. It has to be.'

'Then answer it, Halfdan,' came a shout from the right side of the hall.

81

'What if the lad's a demon in disguise?' said another. 'What if Loki sent him? Beware of his trickery.'

'What's trickery compared to the gods?' snarled Halfdan. 'If this is Odin's watchman, then there will be a sign.'

The warriors waited. When nothing happened the shouting started again.

'Throw the boy out.'

'Send him on his way.'

But the chorus of shouts was interrupted by another loud crash and a huge, long-handled hammer flew across the hall, landing on the table.

'Mjollnir?' gasped Halfdan. 'The thunderer's hammer. Do my eyes deceive me?'

He stared questioningly at Phoenix.

'Is it true? Can you really be the one you claim? Are you Heimdall?'

Phoenix stared at the hammer with almost as much amazement as Halfdan, but finally managed a reply.

'I am Heimdall.'

'Don't believe him, Forkbeard,' protested one man seated at the far end of the table. 'He has an accomplice. That's all, an accomplice lurking outside.'

Halfdan marched to the shattered door and looked out.

'Then the accomplice is fleet of foot. There is nobody here. And there are no footprints in the snow.'

A murmur ran round the hall.

'Leave the lad be,' cried one brave warrior. 'He has been sent by the gods.'

'Yes,' said another. 'It would be blasphemy not to welcome him into our hall.'

Halfdan looked down at the hammer as if in awe of it.

'Is that the verdict of you all?' he asked. 'To leave the boy be?'

Halfdan's question was answered with thunderous acclaim.

'Then take your place at the table, lad,' said the chieftain. 'You're the first representative of the gods to come our way.'

'I'll be happy to accept your hospitality,' said Phoenix. 'One small favour, though. Could my friend join us?'

He indicated Laura, who appeared to be trying to shrink into the floor.

'Very well. You have the blessing of Thor and Odin. She can join us.'

Laura sat down next to Phoenix. The pair of them glanced from the hammer to the shattered door, already being patched with rough planks by two of Halfdan's men. So who *had* thrown the hammer?

3

'So,' said a voice by Phoenix's left shoulder, 'you tell Lord Halfdan that you are Heimdall, watchman of Asgard. The gods have not forsaken us then?'

For all the man's suspicious tone, Phoenix looked up from his plate with some gratitude. He didn't need much of an excuse to stop eating. The gristly meat was swimming in a pool of fat that was congealing into a brown and white swirl. As for the black bread that went with it, the stuff was as tasteless as cardboard and hard enough to file metal.

'This bread,' Phoenix asked. 'What's it made of?'

'Pine-bark,' came the unappetising answer.

'And the meat?'

'Walrus belly.'

Phoenix grimaced.

'Don't turn your nose up. In these dark times that amounts to a feast. Or do you still dine on succulent meats in high Asgard?'

The man who had addressed him with such sarcasm and rescued him from a meal worse than death had been sitting to the right of Halfdan Forkbeard when they first entered the hall.

'Before I tell you anything,' Phoenix replied cautiously, 'may I know who is asking?'

'I am the Jarl's chief counsel. I go by the name of Eirik Bluetooth . . .'

He pulled back his upper lip.

'Though, as you will see, this useless fang is grey rather than blue, the result of a lucky punch by a bruiser of a Night Elf.'

He leaned forward to confide in his listeners.

'That Elf now lies headless in five fathoms of icy water. A rascal's reward.'

He drew a dagger and drove its point into the wood of the table.

'So die all enemies of Skaldheim.'

Laura turned away, but it wasn't in fear of the dagger. Eirik Badbreath might have been a better title for Halfdan's gnarled adviser.

'Well, Eirik Bluetooth,' said Phoenix, ignoring the menacing introduction. 'You know who I am. This is Laura.'

Eirik gave Laura the briefest of glances then fixed Phoenix with his fierce, blue eyes. They glinted with suspicion.

'And what business does the watchman of Asgard have with the men of Skaldheim?'

'The forces of evil are rising,' said Phoenix. 'Loki is about to shake off his chains and lead his legions against Asgard. On the day of Ragnarok, man and god must stand together against him. I am here to summon you to arms.'

Those who overheard stopped what they were doing and stared. One even gathered himself up in his cloak and retreated outside. Phoenix could scarcely have caused more consternation if he had lobbed a grenade into the gathering. For the second time, he had brought silence to the hall of Skaldheim. Eirik waved away the listeners' attention. As the conversation and banter resumed, he leaned closer. His breath was a heady mix of ale, ox-meat, onions and rotting teeth.

'Lower your voice,' he advised. 'The Mischief-Maker strikes no note of terror in my heart. These other souls, however, their horizons are narrow. They give Halfdan Forkbeard unquestioning obedience and live and die in his service to protect Skaldheim from the forces of evil. Don't ask these men to look too high towards the heavens or too far down into the underworld. The Berserkers are simple men. Ale, a fully belly, a warm bed and a good fight. That's all they need to be happy with their lot. As to matters of heaven and hell and the fate of the gods, they're best forgotten.'

'But if they don't fight,' Phoenix replied, 'this whole world will be destroyed. You will be overwhelmed by creatures like the one we encountered.'

'And you come to save us?'

'I come to save your world.'

'You ran into a dead-walker, you say?' Eirik asked, the same expression of suspicion in his eyes.

'Yes,' said Laura. 'Do you see them often?'

'They are the undead, the spawn of Hela, creatures of the Underworld. With the onset of this Age of Evil they swarm across the earth. By now they probably outnumber the living. They serve the Evil One.'

Phoenix felt his stomach clench. He remembered the menace that lay in the circuit boards of the computer.

The Evil One.

A fitting ally for the Gamesmaster.

'Then you will fight?'

'Fight?' Eirik repeated. 'I don't know if there is much fight left in the men of Skaldheim.'

'But you must,' said Phoenix. 'Didn't you hear me? The Evil One is about to rise. He's the one I came to destroy.'

Eirik cut him short, pressing a finger to his lips. He took Phoenix by the sleeve and led him to a corner. Halfdan was watching with interest. Giving his lord a glance, Eirik whispered into Phoenix's ear:

'Loki has spies everywhere. Not all who shelter in the hall of Skaldheim owe allegiance to Forkbeard. So don't go wagging that tongue so freely in future.'

He peered into Phoenix's face.

'A boy who declares to the world that he will kill Loki! Do you not understand his power, the greatness of his malice? You are either very brave or very foolish . . .'

He paused before finishing.

'. . . or in the service of the Evil One.'

'I am neither brave nor foolish,' said Phoenix. 'And I will never serve Loki. You saw the hammer. Surely you know the truth when you see it. I have a mission. I can only complete my quest by cutting out this evil.'

'By the beard of Odin, your trick with the hammer may have convinced these simple souls, but I have witnessed mysteries in my time. I have seen the Valkyries ride, I have seen the unburied dead dance on the storm-tide. I need more proof than this.'

Eirik's eyes shifted from Laura to Phoenix. He picked up the hammer from where it lay on the table.

'Do you expect me to believe that this is truly Mjollnir, the hammer wielded by the thunderer himself?'

'No,' said Phoenix. 'But it is his sign.'

'A sign?'

He scratched his matted beard.

'Maybe it is. I would like nothing better than to believe you. It would be good to take a stand against the Evil One.'

He seemed to put aside his suspicions for a moment.

'What you say has been foretold. The Evil One will rise. Soon giant and demon, wolf and serpent will issue forth and engage in battle on Vigrid Plain. The gods will ride out from great Asgard and join the battle. Then the sun will darken at noon, and heaven and earth will turn red with blood. Good and evil will perish alike in the slaughter and the stars shall vanish from the skies. Now do you understand why I do not want you speaking of such things in the company of these men? It is their grim present . . .'

He cast his arms wide, indicating the raging blizzard.

'. . . their grimmer future too. What man of woman born wishes to face his destiny if it means only blood and fire?'

'But if you know all this, why do you hesitate to fight? What have you got to lose?'

Eirik shook his head.

'Why, because for three winters every soul in Midgard has been shivering behind barred doors. Farmers have broken their ploughshares on the frost-hardened ground. Babes have frozen in their cribs for want of warmth. Everywhere there is greed, law-breaking and the corruption of all faith. How can we trust anyone? Who is to say you were not sent by the Mischief-Maker?'

'Then I will speak to Halfdan Forkbeard.'

'I have fought at Halfdan's side for twenty years. Who do you think he will listen to?'

'So you will hide yourself away here?' asked Phoenix bitterly. 'Like cowards.'

'Skaldheim is a sanctuary. A sacred grove amid the wasting of the Northland. We take our stand against Evil. You cannot shame me with your words, stranger. Prove beyond a shadow of doubt that you serve the cause of the gods. Then and only then will we follow you.'

The fires in the great hall had burned low. Some of the men had gone to their beds, while others slumbered fitfully on their folded arms.

'My liege is about to retire,' said Eirik Bluetooth. 'We will speak again in the morning.'

'But where will we sleep?' asked Laura, casting a suspicious glance at the feasters who were lying sprawled all round the room.

'Where you can,' said Eirik, tossing a pile of rough coverings.

He tugged at an iron ring attached to a wooden hatch.

'You may find some comfort in Lord Halfdan's ale-cellar, though there must be no interfering with his mead casks.'

He leaned forward, leaving them with another sour warning:

'And you will be watched. I will leave you your sword in case you are telling the truth. But one of Halfdan's bodyguard, Ragnar, will keep watch to see that you do not use it for foul means. No treachery, or you will die this very night.'

4

If it was possible, the wind became even stronger in the small hours, booming dismally over the thatched roof and making the timbers grate, while the many draughts that invaded the hall clawed at the sleeping men and made the fire's dying embers glow faintly beneath the grinding rafters. The wind even penetrated to the cellar where Laura and Phoenix lay among the casks of mead and ale. Laura woke from an uneasy sleep, troubled by images of the undead. She was shivering.

'Phoenix,' she whispered, imagining dead-walkers in every shadow. 'Are you awake?'

'Of course I am.'

She threw off her beaver-hide blanket.

'Do you trust that man?'

'Eirik Bluetooth? Yes, I think so.'

'Well, I don't. There is something about him.'

Phoenix laughed.

'Because he mistrusts us, or because he smells?'

'He does reek a bit.'

'I knew it. That's the twenty-first-century girl talking.'

Laura scowled. He wasn't taking her seriously. She changed the subject.

'Is it safe to talk?'

'I don't think anyone is listening.'

'There's one thing I don't understand. Where *did* the hammer come from? It's not like we're used to getting help when we play the game. It couldn't have really been from Thor, could it?'

Phoenix shook his head.

'I just don't know. There is one possibility.'

Laura waited.

'Andreas.'

'Are you telling me we were saved by a dead man?'

'I hear his voice.'

Laura shook her head.

'But this wasn't a voice. Voices don't throw hammers.'

She brought her arm down to illustrate her point.

'This was an enormous sledgehammer and somebody threw it. Believe me, Phoenix, we're not the only players in the game.'

Some time later Phoenix was woken, first by a dull thud then by a scraping noise. It was coming from above. He wasn't imagining it, somebody was opening the hatch of the mead-cellar. He heard the wooden staircase creak. Somebody was coming down. His skin began to prickle.

Why now, in the dead of night?

Reassuring himself that Laura was asleep, he closed his hand round the hilt of the longsword and waited. Another creak. Whoever it was, they were descending slowly.

What do they want?

Phoenix had been sleeping on his right side with his back to the staircase. Holding his breath and shifting his weight bit by bit, he eased himself over, until he could see the dark figure out of the corner of his eye. The fires in the hall had burned down low and it was impossible to make out any details. Phoenix watched the man's approach and his heartbeat quickened. There was no innocent explanation for this furtive movement. It was at that moment that Laura woke up.

She too saw the dark figure and cried out. The intruder

reacted by jumping the rest of the way down the staircase and drawing a dagger. It was time to act. Phoenix threw back the pelt under which he had been sleeping and brandished his longsword. Blade struck blade and a desperate struggle began, boy and man crashing about in near total darkness, slashing at one another. Phoenix was hard-pressed to hold off his assailant and the points bracelet clicked away at his wrist.

'Phoenix!' cried Laura as he rolled away from one slashing thrust.

His attacker drove a boot into Phoenix's ribs. Phoenix felt the breath knocked out of him and clutched his side. He looked up in pain as his opponent's dagger flashed. He just succeeded in locking the hilt of his sword against the blade.

'Who sent you?' he panted.

He already knew the answer. This had to be Loki's man, and he was slashing and hacking with a fury that had Phoenix on the back foot. Seeing Phoenix hurt and falling back, Laura rolled a mead barrel into the attacker's path. It earned Phoenix a brief respite and he threw himself forward, sword swinging. For the first time, he was fighting on equal terms.

'Now you are going to tell me who sent you,' said Phoenix.

But the fight ended as quickly as it had begun, the attacker slumping to his knees with a groan.

'What happened?' asked Laura. 'Did you . . . ?'

Phoenix shook his head.

'I wanted him alive.'

He examined the body.

'I don't understand. I didn't touch him.'

'No,' came a voice. 'I did.'

It was Halfdan, holding a firebrand in his left hand.

'Somebody woke me up. I don't know who it was, he was gone back into the shadows before I could open my eyes. But believe me, you have a friend here, watchman.'

Laura and Phoenix exchanged glances. Meanwhile Halfdan

shone the firebrand over the dead man and pulled the great axe Bloodletter from between his shoulder blades.

'A traveller,' he said, 'to whom we had given shelter. He slew Ragnar, my faithful bodyguard, to get at you. So this is how he repays my hospitality.'

Eirik appeared and examined the body.

'Maybe you were telling the truth all along. Do you have any idea why he would want to kill you?'

Phoenix examined the man.

'Here.'

There was a mark like a tattoo on the man's neck. It was in the shape of a wolf. Halfdan frowned.

'What's wrong?'

'The assassin bears the mark of the Evil One. This is the brand of Loki. These are evil days indeed.'

'I've seen something like this before,' said Phoenix. 'It is worn by our enemy's disciples. It gives him power over their thoughts and actions.'

'Loki?'

Phoenix had meant the Gamesmaster, but he wasn't about to contradict Halfdan. For the purposes of the game, it amounted to the same thing.

'The Evil One knows we're here,' said Phoenix. 'He will do anything to destroy us. You have to act, Lord Halfdan.'

Eirik inspected the wolf tattoo and whispered something in Halfdan's ear.

'If Loki sent this assassin,' said Halfdan, 'then maybe you were right about the dead-walker. This may well be the second attempt on your lives. In the morning we will climb the hill and take a look at the shrine. Try to get some sleep.'

But he was asking too much. Neither Phoenix nor Laura closed their eyes again that night.

5

By the white light of early morning, Phoenix and Laura led Halfdan Forkbeard and his men up the windswept hillside to the shrine. In the dawnlight, Phoenix could see clearly the runes and the creatures of the Northland: serpents, wolves, bears, and the sacred raven, the bird of Odin. The warriors' beards and hair were matted with grease and their tunics were heavily stained where the ale had spilled down their chests. Most were nursing ferocious hangovers.

'And this is where you saw your dead-walker?' asked Eirik Bluetooth as they reached the squat, grey building.

'There,' said Laura, 'on the other side of the wall. It was hanging from the tree.'

By speaking out so freely, she set off much sullen muttering among Halfdan's followers. The Berserkers weren't used to such boldness in a female.

'Asgard must be a stranger place than I had ever believed,' said Eirik, addressing Phoenix. 'Where boys keep vigil and womenfolk talk out of turn.'

Laura's eyes flashed angrily. There was something about this man with his reeking breath and his discoloured tooth. She thought of the would-be assassin from the night before and wondered how many more traitors there were in Skaldheim. How she would have liked to really talk out of turn! But she knew better than to provoke the Berserkers to anger, and said no more.

'Why, it wouldn't surprise me if you didn't set infants up as kings!' bellowed Halfdan, blissfully unaware of Laura's thoughts.

'What Laura says is true,' Phoenix insisted. 'There *was* a body hanging from that tree. It came alive and . . .'

'A body,' scoffed one sceptical soul. 'Now we know the boy is lying. Sacrifice occurs every ninth year, and it is barely a twelvemonth since the last festival.'

'You allow human sacrifice!' gasped Laura, horrified.

'The rites have not been practised for many years,' Halfdan explained. 'In better times they fell into disuse. But when the time of cold and want fell upon our land, the demand for blood became irresistible.'

'But how could you?' Laura demanded, oblivious to the angry looks of the men.

'Stop this talk,' Halfdan commanded. 'This shrine was standing when the world was new, and I will not have its traditions dishonoured. Those who died here were obeying the will of the gods.'

He glared at Phoenix.

'Either you control the wench's mouth, or you will find our goodwill towards you has gone too, watchman of Asgard.'

Phoenix glanced at Laura wondering how exactly to persuade her, but there was no need. She nodded briefly. They were in no position to argue. Meanwhile, Eirik Bluetooth was leading the way into the shrine. In the light of day it looked harmless enough.

'There is no sign of your dead-walker,' he said, examining the ancient oak. 'And as for it hanging from this branch . . .' He ran his fingers over the bark. 'Why, there is no rope and no sign of chafing on the bark.'

His suspicions of the night before returned.

'Maybe it *was* all invention,' said Eirik, darkness clouding his face. 'A tall tale to wheedle your way into our company.'

The suggestion raised a growl of hostility among the warriors.

'Can it be possible?' mused Halfdan Forkbeard. 'Did you make it all up?'

'You mean the same way I made up the assassin?' asked Phoenix. 'Or the way I made up the hammer?'

He was facing the men, waving his arms to reinforce the point, when Laura screamed.

'Laura?'

'Phoenix. Look!'

Phoenix turned to see something that made his heart miss a beat. The oak had been transformed into a giant, malformed hand. It reminded him of the hands of the undead. Fleshless, the last remains of skin were peeling back to expose earth-blackened bone. More importantly, it was moving, and the branches that had been so hideously transformed into fingers were pinning Halfdan's Berserkers against the stone walls. Horror was printed on their faces.

'Very well then, watchman,' said Halfdan. 'We believe your tale. Now tell me, what are we to make of this witchcraft?'

'I don't know, Halfdan. I . . .'

But his admission of ignorance had a dramatic effect on the tree. Or at least, his voice did. All five of its finger-branches turned towards him. They seemed to be reaching for him.

'It wants you, boy,' said Halfdan.

The finger pointed to the north.

'What's going on?' asked Eirik.

The palm flattened. For a moments nothing happened. The onlookers exchanged glances. Some fell back in terror.

'What are we meant to make of that?' asked Halfdan once more.

But the hand hadn't finished. A tongue of flame sprang from the palm. Something moved within, a serpent's scales.

'By the All-father!' cried Halfdan.

Then, in the heart of the flame, a figure appeared. Tall and lean, he had a gaunt face, framed by hair as red as flame. And the eyes were sharp and alive, like fires. Phoenix recognized him immediately. Adams. But the Berserkers' reaction surprised him. It wasn't a boy from another world they saw.

'Do you know him?' asked Phoenix.

Eirik met his gaze, but it was Halfdan who spoke:

'The one you see is known throughout the Northland. His features are carved into every rune-stone for miles around. We are looking upon the Father of Lies. That is the Evil One, Loki himself.'

Then the flame seemed to collapse in on itself and disintegrated into a mass of black shapes. Dozens of crows were rising into the sky in a swirling black mist.

'Crows,' snarled Halfdan. 'It is three long years since we saw the raven take wing. Odin is besieged in Asgard and his holy bird is missing from our skies. Bad times indeed.'

'Loki is risen,' said Eirik, wrapping himself in his cloak and walking off down the hill.

In muttering groups, the Berserkers retreated to the security and shelter of their longhouse. For a few minutes Phoenix and Laura remained behind, staring at the oak tree which had returned to its original form.

'These men are terrified,' said Phoenix. 'I don't know how we'll ever raise them to fight. I don't like the way things are going.'

'We've faced danger before,' said Laura. 'You're not telling me this is worse, are you?'

'Maybe.'

'But how?'

'It's Adams. In *The Legendeer, Part One* he was a bit player. By *Part Two* he had become part-monster. Now he takes the role of the Evil One himself. What's happening?'

Laura didn't even attempt an answer.

'Listen,' she said.

They could hear the sound of raised voices. By the time Phoenix and Laura reached the doorway, a furious row had engulfed the hall of Halfdan Forkbeard.

'It's him, the unshaven boy who claims to represent the gods,' argued one man. 'He has brought evil upon Skaldheim.'

This was immediately rebutted by another:

'And did he bring three fatal winters on the land? Did he make our crops lie barren in the ground? Did he set brother against brother, father against son? Don't blame the boy. Blame the Father of Lies.'

'I agree,' said another. 'The lad claims to be Heimdall. What if he is? Will we go against the will of Asgard?'

'Heimdall?' scoffed another. 'This whelp?'

'Does it matter?' asked the second speaker. 'Loki is behind all that is sick in this land. I say we smash the Evil One's followers before his power grows.'

'Enough,' cried Halfdan, raising his arms to quell the furious debate. Phoenix and Laura looked hopefully in his direction. He would know what to do.

'We will not fall out among ourselves,' he thundered.

Then he dashed Phoenix and Laura's hopes.

'What we saw at the shrine was an omen. We will not be tempted into rash decisions. We hold fast in our stronghold of Skaldheim. We will not retreat, nor will we run headlong into his clutches. But let the Mischief-Maker come knocking at our door then, believe me, he will have his battle.'

Laura glanced at Phoenix. He was horrified. This was it, the endgame, the time of reckoning, and all Halfdan could say was: *sit tight.*

'Is this what your Berserkers stand for?' he cried indignantly. 'Skulking in their hall?'

'Watch your tongue, boy,' snarled Eirik. 'You strain our hospitality.'

He and his men had all assumed the same sullen pose, hunched over the great table, heads sunk into their massive shoulders.

'No!' cried Phoenix. 'Knock me down if you wish, but I'll say my piece first. You boast about your exploits, men of Skaldheim, how many dead-walkers you have slain, how many blades you have broken on the skulls of your foes. But I don't see fighters. You may sing of great deeds, but when was the last time you rode into battle?'

Laura watched him striding the length of the hall, darting accusing glances at the frowning warriors. He had shrugged off all thoughts of defeat. The boy was growing into a man before her eyes.

'Look at you.'

He picked up a drinking horn and flung it against the wall.

'What are you good for, men of Skaldheim?'

'Take care, lad,' warned Eirik. 'You go too far.'

'Yes,' agreed a tall, lean wolf of a man who wore a patch over his left eye. 'Treat us with respect, or I'll come over there and stop that runaway mouth of yours.'

'Do it then,' shouted Phoenix. 'Don't just talk about it. Do it!'

Andvar reacted by reaching for his weapon.

'No,' said Halfdan. 'There will be no fighting in this hall.'

He stepped between them.

'Save your courage for our enemies.'

He turned to Phoenix.

'When this boy demanded that we bear arms against Loki, Father of Lies, we turned our backs on him. It was too soon for battle, we said.'

He indicated the giant cloth that hung at the end of the hall.

'But when will we rally to the raven banner? When will we fight, warrior brothers? *When?*'

He took his place at Phoenix's side.

'Do we want to live forever?' he demanded. 'In a draughty hall, sheltering from the wind's blast. Do we want to grow old hiding ourselves in Skaldheim?' He forced them to look at themselves. 'Like this?'

A murmur of agreement ran through the ranks of the Berserkers.

He turned to Phoenix.

'If we follow you, watchman,' he asked. 'Can you lead us to Vigrid where good and evil must contend?'

Phoenix heard the whispered voice in his head.

The way is straight for the Legendeer.

He nodded.

'Yes, I can find the way.'

Halfdan immediately sprang onto the table, ripping the raven banner from the wall and waving it over his head.

'Will we cower beneath this roof like craven curs? Will we accept this living death?'

The eyes of Halfdan Forkbeard blazed fiercely through the feeble dawnlight, bright with indignation.

'Or will we fight?'

He got his answer in the form of a thunderous roar that shook the rafters of the hall. But not all joined in. Watching suspiciously from the back was the one-eyed man, Andvar.

6

A world away, Christina Graves was standing behind her husband, looking over his shoulder. Her eyes were fixed on the computer screen. Time was frozen around them. Clocks didn't tick, the tv screen was in freeze-frame, advertising the game that was due in the shops in a matter of hours. Even dust motes were caught motionless. The only time that moved was the time of the game.

'My poor Phoenix,' Mum murmured. 'Isn't there anything we can do?'

'Nothing,' said John Graves. 'You know that, Christina. Now that they've entered the world of the game, they are beyond our reach. It is all up to Phoenix now.'

'But he's just a boy.'

The mother in her was talking.

'No,' Dad replied. 'That's where you're wrong. You of all people should know. He has a destiny, like Andreas before him. You have stood here beside me twice before, witnessing his adventures. Worlds that would drive any normal person insane are like a second home to him. If anybody can end this madness, it is Phoenix.'

'You really believe that?'

John Graves remembered his son's previous desperate struggles. Burying his doubts, he turned to his wife with a reassuring smile.

'I know it.'

'Is it true what Eirik Bluetooth says?' asked Andvar, reining in his grey stallion beside Phoenix and Laura. 'You are leading us to sacred Vigrid. You take us to the land that lies beneath the home of the gods?'

Andvar wasn't asking, he was *interrogating*.

'Yes,' said Phoenix, hunching forward in his saddle. 'That's where the final battle will take place. Vigrid plain.'

Laura saw Andvar's eyes burning into Phoenix. Something about his expression unsettled her.

'I wonder,' said Andvar slowly. 'Are you truly sent by the gods, or by the Evil One?'

'What?' cried Phoenix. 'You still mistrust us?'

Andvar's hand moved to the jewelled dagger that was hanging from his belt.

'Somehow you have pulled the wool over Halfdan's eyes, convinced him you were sent by the gods, but I can see through you. Ours is a harsh and brutal land. Betrayal is our bread and treachery our wine. I trust nobody but my comrades in arms.'

A fight was only prevented by the arrival of Eirik Bluetooth.

'What is this?' he asked. 'Sheathe your weapons. We're only half a day's ride out of Skaldheim and already you are at each other's throats.'

'How do we know this isn't a trap?' snarled Andvar. 'We follow him to Vigrid, to face who knows what odds.'

'We know nothing,' Eirik replied. 'Only that the Mischief-Maker is about to rise and Odin's warriors must stand and be counted.'

With a scowl, Andvar spurred his horse to a canter and left them behind.

'We are in your debt, Eirik,' said Phoenix.

'Andvar is quick to anger,' said Eirik shortly. 'Try not to give him cause.'

102

With that he rode ahead, leaving them to consider what had just happened.

'Doesn't anybody trust us?' said Laura.

'Not wholeheartedly,' Phoenix replied. 'Would you?'

'If these are our friends,' said Laura, 'what are our enemies going to be like?'

Phoenix smiled.

'They're all we've got. If we are to win, we will need their help.'

Laura was about to say something in reply when suddenly her horse reared.

'Phoenix, help me!'

Her mount was kicking up clouds of powdery snow with its hooves. For a few moments the snow-cloud hit the ground around them and the rest of the Berserker column. Then Phoenix saw the reason for the horse's panic. A few steps ahead of them, the ground was cracking. A huge, scaly shape twisted in the fissure.

'Dead-Biter!' cried Halfdan Forkbeard.

Eirik rode back and helped Phoenix gain control of Laura's terrified mount.

'Dead-Biter?' asked Phoenix.

'Aye,' Eirik replied. 'The foul serpent that gnaws endlessly on the Tree of Life, the creature of emptiness and forever night. It brings the walkers.'

As if to confirm his words, the undead began to rise from the broken ground, first in dozens then in scores.

'Draw swords,' bellowed Halfdan. 'Defend yourselves.'

But the dead-walkers made no move forward. They seemed content to form up in foul, flesh-creeping ranks.

'What are they doing?' asked Laura.

'I don't know,' Eirik answered, surveying their grisly lines, 'but I don't like it.'

'There's your answer,' said Phoenix, pointing to a high ridge.

A tall, flame-haired figure was standing on a rocky peak, looking down at them. A pack of wolves prowled round him.

'Do you know me, Halfdan Forkbeard?' he asked.

'Aye, I know you, Loki, Father of Mischief.'

He pointed at the dead-walkers.

'And I know your evil spawn.'

Loki smiled.

'Is this your army, Halfdan? Is it with this motley crew that you intend to stop me?'

Phoenix watched the blazing eyes roving over the Berserkers, counting the warriors.

'There are no gods to help you, Forkbeard. Even now an army of giants is laying siege to the walls of Asgard. The great wolf Fenris howls before its battlements. Surt the flamer unleashes his fire-demons on the Asa-gods. And who is there to relieve great Odin and his sky-lords? Why, boozy Halfdan and his pot-bellied Berserkers!'

He chuckled at the thought.

'Do you really expect to reach Vigrid with this ragged band? And what will you do there, a few hundred mortals against my demon army? Return home, Halfdan, to where the ale is strong and the meat is tender. This isn't your fight.'

Halfdan took a step forward and gave his reply:

'A long time ago a boy was taken to the holy ground of Vigrid. He stood proudly beneath the raven banner of Odin and he was shown the rainbow bridge, Bifrost. His father foretold the fall of heaven and he grieved. To comfort him in the darkest moment of his childhood, he was given a golden ring and told to wear it until the day that mortal men would take their stand against the legions of Evil. I am that boy, Lord Loki.'

He raised his fist, flaunting the ring in defiance.

'And I wear the ring today. I will not turn back from my destiny.'

Loki grinned, gesturing to his demon supporters to hold their ground.

'A pretty speech, Jarl of Skaldheim, but it will take more than your raggle-taggle band to thwart me. Let's see if you sing such a brave tune when the time comes to fight.'

He looked at Phoenix for the first time.

'And you're the one they follow. What's the name you go by now, Legendeer? Heimdall, is it? The one who must face me on the day of judgement. The game is in its closing stages. Are you ready for the last throw of the dice?'

Phoenix thought of hundreds of thousands, maybe millions of copies of *Warriors of the Raven*, just waiting to be bought, and imagined the havoc they would wreak. He roared his reply.

'I'm ready.'

Then he glanced at Halfdan.

'We all are.'

7

It was close to nightfall when Halfdan gave the order to set up camp. The Berserkers had ridden all day into the teeth of a piercing Arctic wind and men and horses were exhausted. Many were wondering why Loki hadn't attacked. His sinister game of cat and mouse made them nervous.

'Get those tents up!' barked Eirik, relaying his chief's curt command. 'I don't care how tired you are, you can't rest without shelter. Half of us could perish on a night like this.'

The Berserkers set about their task in silence; dark, sullen men labouring in the winter twilight. Laura had her eye on Eirik. She was thinking of the assassin who had attacked them in Halfdan's hall, a man with a wolf tattoo.

'I still don't trust him.'

Phoenix shook his head.

'It's Andvar we have to watch. If anyone serves the Games-master, it's him.'

Then the crows came back.

Nobody noticed them at first, dark scraps flickering against the greying sky. Laura was the one to realize.

'Phoenix. Something's happening.'

She answered his questioning look by pointing to the north. There, wheeling lazily over a ridge, were a few score of the shrilly cawing birds. Phoenix shuddered despite himself.

'Dark,' he said, 'like death.'

Laura stared at the crows.

'What made you say that?' she asked, trembling. She wasn't sure what caused the gust of fright, the massing birds or Phoenix's words.

'The crow belongs to the dark places,' Phoenix replied, watching the birds gathering. 'It is an omen. A harbinger of ill fortune.'

Within moments the few dozen crows had grown to several hundred, some clustered on the wind-blasted pines that clung uneasily to the thin soil, others on the wing above the sprouting encampment.

'Phoenix, there's definitely something wrong here.'

'I know.'

He was speaking in a monotone, as if bewitched. He and Laura weren't alone in sensing the menace. The Berserkers had stopped pulling on their guy ropes. All eyes turned towards the growing mass of birds.

'Heimdall,' murmured Eirik. 'What is this?'

Phoenix turned slowly in a circle, following the line of settling birds. The creeping twilight went on forever and it was all birds. The sky, the land, the air itself was growing crow-dark. The points bracelet started to click. Phoenix's score was falling.

'I know what's happening here,' he said in a voice muffled with fear. 'We're being surrounded.'

'What?'

Surrounded!

The secret speaker was whispering a warning.

'Stop them,' yelled Phoenix, suddenly alive to the danger. 'We can't afford to let them form a circle.'

'Why not?'

'Believe me, it would be bad for us.'

Eirik didn't need any more convincing.

'To horse!' he ordered. 'Stop the birds from forming a circle.'

Andvar was the first into the saddle, galloping forward and swinging his Skull-crusher at the carpet of crows.

'Yaagh!'

His voice raked the dusk, hoarse and brave.

'Yaagh!'

Then the entire troop of horse was thundering across the frosty ground, scattering the birds to flight. It wasn't a moment too soon. To the north, where the crows were at their thickest, the air was choked with the fluttering of thousands of wings. It was a strange sound, an irregular snapping and clattering. But amidst the shifting, rippling chatter of bone and feather there was another beat. Something deep and repetitive, a distinct and recognizable pounding.

'What is that?' asked Laura, her heart skipping inside her chest. 'It sounds familiar. Like . . .'

The low, concealed beat continued, often completely swallowed up in the roaring of the Berserkers and the tide of wing-beats. But still Laura listened, trying to distinguish what she'd heard.

'Phoenix,' she asked. 'What did you mean? Why do we have to break the circle?'

'It's Andreas. He's warning us.'

Laura stared at him for a moment, then turned towards the main flock.

'What *is* that sound?'

She almost shouted the question. She was angry with herself. Why couldn't she put a name to it?

The Berserkers were riding up and down the frozen ground, roaring and waving their arms, scattering the crows wherever they landed. Eirik led the way. He was doing anything he could to prevent the birds settling. Andvar was just as keen and loud. The remaining warriors did their bit, but with less enthusiasm.

They were keeping the circle open, but their efforts fell short of shifting the main flock to their north. It was forming a solid mass, a swelling mound of birds. No, not a single mound. Ten, a dozen, twenty black shapes.

Like . . .

Like the forms of men.

'Of course,' cried Phoenix as the crow-blackness became legs, arms, hands, a head. 'Halfdan, Eirik. The crows. They're not just birds. They are part of the darkness. If we allow them to settle they will make dead-walkers.'

'Hear that?' bellowed Halfdan. 'It's a trick. Dead-walkers. The Mischief-Maker thought to encircle us with dead-walkers.'

Until then the Berserkers had been following Eirik and Andvar's example only half-heartedly. Now that they understood their enemy, they set about their winged tormentors with renewed fury, slashing and hacking at the dark shapes. But if they were beginning to disperse the birds to the south and east, to the north an unbroken phalanx was forming. A regiment of dead-walkers. Suddenly, in the sky above, Loki appeared riding a great eagle.

'My power is growing, Legendeer. Surprise, surpulse!'

A Berserker's arrow just missed him, but the eagle swooped low.

'The dark power is rising,' he said. 'Soon you will meet the one you fear.'

The Gamesmaster.

The undead legions continued to advance. Laura glimpsed the points bracelet and its falling score.

'We have to fight this,' cried Phoenix, 'without delay.'

'To arms!' bawled Halfdan, throwing back his heavy cloak to reveal a chain-mail jacket. 'This is something we know, something we can fight. Archers, draw up your lines.'

At the first volley of arrows the as yet unformed dead-walkers exploded in a deafening tumult of sound. The air was filled with the shrieking of thousands, tens of thousands of the creatures.

'That's it,' cried Phoenix jubilantly. 'The transformation isn't complete. Hit the dead-walkers before they're fully formed.'

Then the shafts sang, and each time their arrowheads thudded into a mound of crows the tattered black shapes spiralled into the thickening gloom.

'Strain your arms, lads,' shouted Halfdan encouragingly. 'Keep your aim true and win the fight.'

With a final volley, the archers dispersed the last of the dead-walkers and roared their triumph at the blizzard of crows. Phoenix and Laura joined their celebrations. But their victory shout had barely left their throats when another voice crackled through the night.

'Think you've won, do you, Halfdan?'

It was Loki himself.

'Surely you know better?'

'Where is he?' asked Laura.

Phoenix could just make out an eerie glare in an oak grove. It was a violent and destructive flame, leaping and licking at the tree-tops, sending showers of sparks into the night sky. Loki's voice came from the heart of the blaze.

'You want a *real* fight?'

He paused as the earth began to shake.

'Then fight this.'

The muffled heartbeat which had worried Laura so much was now deafening. While the fiery light flared and the frozen ground cracked, a huge serpent body could be seen arching through the gaping earth. It was the monster's heart she'd heard.

Dead-Biter.

Moments later armies of the undead began to spill in countless thousands from the gap.

'By the gods of Asgard!' gasped Halfdan. 'There are hundreds, thousands. Never have I seen so many.'

As the words left his lips Loki added his comment.

'Worried, Legendeer? Surprise, surprise.'

The sky above was black with crows, the hills around them a grey carpet of dead-walkers. The noose was closing.

8

'Don't let them complete the circle!' cried Phoenix instinctively. 'We've got to break out.'

The Berserkers rode at breakneck pace. After a furious fight, they smashed through the dead-walkers' ranks, but there was to be no respite for Halfdan's battered army. Just minutes after the break-out, Andvar had returned from a scouting mission to the top of the nearest peak with ominous news.

'I saw them, Halfdan, down in the valley.'

'How far?'

'A league. Maybe less. I could sense their fury even from such a distance. Their numbers are growing all the time. And they have dragons now, and other creatures of the night such as I have never seen before.'

A murmur of dismay ran through the ranks. It was indeed the rising of the dark powers.

Ragnarok was at hand.

'Enough,' barked Halfdan, feeling the spirit draining out of his men. 'We may have been badly mauled, but we won't go to our graves moaning like cattle.'

It was only then, as Halfdan marshalled his fearful warriors, that Eirik Bluetooth noticed the change that had come over Phoenix.

'What ails you, watchman?'

Phoenix was slumped in his saddle, his head hanging to one side, his eyes half closed.

'He's hurt,' said Laura.

This time nobody turned to stare at her. The arrogance of the Berserkers had been shattered by their near-defeat at the hands of the dead-walkers.

'We have to get him down.'

As if confirming Laura's words, Phoenix started to slip from his horse. It was only Andvar's strong right hand that prevented him falling.

'Lift him down,' Halfdan ordered. 'Gently does it. Mind his head.'

While Laura knelt anxiously beside the half-conscious Phoenix, Halfdan dispatched more scouts.

'No fires,' he ordered. 'We snatch what rest we can and trust our sentries to alert us to any attack. Don't unbuckle your weapons, or even take off your boots.'

'What's that, Halfdan?' asked Andvar. 'Do you really think we could sleep after what we have seen this day?'

Ignoring Andvar, Halfdan continued; 'We will ride at first light. We must reach Vigrid and open a way for the gods to ride out of Asgard. It is our only hope, and theirs too. But if the Evil One moves before then we must too. We cannot fight him alone. The gods need us, but we need them more.'

'What is your plan?' asked Eirik.

Halfdan took his adviser to one side.

'To live to see the morning,' he replied grimly. 'Why, do you have anything to add?'

'Nothing, ring-giver,' said Eirik flatly.

Overhearing their gloomy exchange, Laura felt her heart go cold. Nobody spoke after that. Andvar made Phoenix as comfortable as he could, and Laura lay next to him, watching as he tossed and turned in his trance-like sleep. She couldn't take her eyes off the points bracelet. The score was ominously low. The game was almost lost.

'You're going to be all right,' she said: 'You've got to be.'

She tried to stay awake, but weariness soon overcame her. To begin with she dozed a little, before snapping to attention, then grew heavy-lidded once more.

Eventually she was unable to keep her eyes open and slipped into a fitful sleep. This time, it was her turn to dream. She saw the crows circling, then gather into hideous, mis-shapen statues. She ran round and round the circle begging to be allowed out, but the statues turned their eyeless faces on her, closing in on her, tightening the circle like a noose.

'No!'

She sat bolt upright and saw Andvar and Halfdan looking at her.

'Sorry,' she said. 'I had a bad dream.'

Andvar simply snorted and rolled over, but Halfdan gave a sympathetic smile.

'There will be many bad dreams before daybreak,' he said. 'We have never seen the dead-walkers in such numbers before. The tramp of evil shakes the earth. The Mischief-Maker's time has come.'

'We're beaten, aren't we?' asked Laura.

Just a day before, her question would have been dismissed scornfully by the proud Viking lord. But Halfdan didn't reply at all. He buried his face in his jacket and clapped his gloved hands together against the bitter cold of the night.

'Halfdan,' Laura began. 'Is there . . . ?'

Her question was cut short by a shout in the darkness.

The Berserkers were on their feet in seconds, drawing their swords and battle-axes.

'Who goes there?' cried Halfdan.

One of the sentries replied, 'It's riders, my lord.'

All eyes turned towards the thud of hooves. Moments later two riders galloped into view.

'Lord Halfdan,' shouted one, his voice a mixture of excite-ment and despair. 'There is something you must see.'

Halfdan mounted his horse.

'Eirik,' said Laura, 'will you watch Phoenix? I want to go with them.'

'Yes, I'll watch the lad. You go.'

She smiled. How wrong she had been about him. She joined Halfdan's party. They followed the scouts into the darkness with a growing sense of dread. As they rode up the slope and through a screen of pines, Laura became aware of hundreds of lights flickering in the lowlands around them, their gleam penetrating through the dense woods like searchlight beams.

'What's that glow?' she asked.

She was answered as they rode out onto open ground and looked down from the brow of the hill.

'By the beard of Odin!'

'We're surrounded,' cried Andvar. 'And this time there's no breaking the circle.'

Laura gazed in dismay at the enemy hordes camped at the foot of the hill. Many of the ghoulish figures were completely enveloped in flame.

'But how did they surround us without our hearing?'

'We are dealing with the undead here,' Halfdan said. 'They do not speak to give orders, or to reassure one another as mortal men do. They are soulless. They simply obey their master's orders.'

'But why the fires?' asked Laura. 'If they're the undead, why do they need warmth?'

'They don't,' said Halfdan. 'The fires are for our benefit. The Mischief-Maker wishes to break our sleep and plant the seed of terror. They have set their fires to tell us that we will die in the morning.'

'And will we?' asked Laura.

Halfdan gestured at the ocean of firelight.

'Nothing,' he replied, 'is so certain.'

115

Level Ten
Ragnarok

1

John and Christina Graves watched transfixed as their son lay semiconscious, his head pillowed on the coarse material of a warrior's jacket.

'Surely it can't end like this,' said Mum, pressing her fingers against Phoenix's image on the computer screen.

For once, there were no reassuring words from her husband.

'John?'

'Christina, I'm afraid,' he said finally. 'Not once in either of the other games were the odds so heavily stacked against him. The game seems different this time. This is a world where even gods can die.'

No sooner were the words out of his mouth than the computer screen started to fill with a myriad of numbers, the familiar maelstrom of threes, sixes and nines. Then, from out of the jumble of numerals, came a message, direct and chilling:

This is the endgame. The time of my victory. In a matter of hours the wall between my world and yours will be destroyed and we shall meet.

Phoenix's parents looked into the numbers. For the first time, they saw them decoded.

'It's the Gamesmaster,' said Dad. 'He thinks he's won.'

It was always going to be this way. I chose my terrain well. The Norse myths. Where man and god are both mortal. Where the power of Evil can triumph. Ragnarok the final battle is about to dawn. All my enemies will be slain on Vigrid plain, the Legendeer among them. The gateway between the worlds will open and I will be made whole, no longer a phantom but a living, vengeful being. I have my vessel, the means by which I will live again. Soon the Gamesmaster will stride the universe, master of the many worlds.

With that, the numbers cleared. Phoenix's parents looked on, not speaking, paralysed by the knowledge that the Gamesmaster had won. Then came new terror. A shadow fell over Phoenix as he lay unprotected.

'Wake up,' cried Mum, 'Phoenix, before it's too late.'

2

Phoenix was gradually coming to his senses. His body ached, but he was more concerned with the figure standing over him. He could see somebody, silhouetted against the first rays of the rising sun, looking down at him. At first Phoenix was unable to speak. He was struggling to throw off a crushing weariness. Finally he uttered a few words:

'Who's there? Laura?'

But the blurred shape was too big to be a teenage girl. Phoenix strained to focus his eyes. He saw a beard, smelt the reek of rancid breath.

'Eirik?'

There was no reply.

'Eirik Bluetooth, is that you?'

Thank goodness. A friend.

But there didn't seem anything in the least friendly about this presence. Phoenix hauled himself into a sitting position. He was starting to see clearly. Eirik was leaning over, scratching distractedly at his neck. Icy currents rippled through Phoenix's veins.

'What are you doing?'

Then he saw the dagger in the Northman's hand, and the scratching took on a sinister meaning. He realized with horror that he had been a fool to trust Eirik. He had been warned and now he was lying defenceless at Eirik's feet.

'Laura was right!'

Eirik spoke for the first time.

'The girl asked me to watch over you.'

He chuckled, seeming to see the funny side.

'I, the demon-lord's man, watching over the watchman!'

Phoenix tried to cry out, the Eirik clamped a rough hand over his mouth.

'Our brave Berserkers are too preoccupied with the Evil One's legions to listen to you.'

Phoenix could feel a dull ache gnawing into his back and legs. He was hurt and exhausted. He couldn't fight back.

'This won't be hard to explain,' hissed Eirik. 'Few of the men ever really trusted you. It won't be difficult to convince them that you were an assassin and a traitor all along. Now Halfdan's trusted adviser has exposed you.'

He raised the dagger to strike. Phoenix closed his eyes, expecting the blow. A moment later, instead of the dagger's thrust, he was flung backwards by Eirik's body falling heavily on him. He screamed and tried in vain to fight off the clumsy attack. But Eirik wasn't doing anything. In fact, he was a dead weight. What *was* he doing?

'Are you all right?' said a boy's voice. 'He didn't hurt you, did he?'

Phoenix finally crawled free. He pulled back the Berserker's long hair and saw the wolf tattoo. Eirik had been Loki's man all along. Tears of relief streamed down Phoenix's cheeks. Above him stood a boy about his own age, blond and blue-eyed, the sledgehammer that had felled the traitor clenched in his fists.

'Who are you?' asked Phoenix.

He recognized the sledgehammer.

'You're the one,' he said. 'The one who came to our aid in Halfdan's hall.'

'I threw the hammer. I couldn't think of anything else to do. It was me that woke Halfdan too. I saw the assassin kill the guard. I came back for the hammer after you'd left Skald-heim.'

Then the scales fell from Phoenix's eyes.

'Of course! You must be Jon.'

The newcomer nodded and held out a hand to Phoenix.

'Jon Jonsson.'

'But how?'

'Dad didn't pack everything to send away. He couldn't bring himself to do it. He decided he needed to keep some in-surance, hang onto proof that what he said was true. Your friend Adams should have checked the box properly. I came across the PR suit and the back-up disc by accident. The moment I found out there was a way back into the game, I knew I had to help you.'

Phoenix wiped away his tears.

'But why didn't you let on? Why be so secretive?'

'I didn't plan to keep you in the dark. It just happened that way. I found the stuff that Dad had stashed away. I used them secretly on my own PC. But I had to choose my moments carefully, or my parents would find out. They were scared enough without me adding to their worries. And I couldn't stay long or they would know.'

Phoenix chuckled.

'You needn't have worried about the time,' he said. 'When you enter the game, time freezes in our world. If they weren't in the same room as the computer when you entered they would be frozen too. They would never know you were gone.'

'Is this true?'

Phoenix nodded.

'I should know. This is the third of the myth games I have played.'

'So I didn't need to go back?'

Phoenix shook his head. 'No. But how could you pass back

121

and forth between the worlds? Once you're inside you're trapped. That's the way it has always been before.'

Jon shrugged.

'Nobody told me that. I just came and went as I pleased.'

Phoenix frowned again.

'Unless . . . Of course, the Gamesmaster can't hold you here the way he has me and Laura because *he doesn't even know you've entered*. You're an unknown player. You've got a freedom I never had.'

Jon leaned on the hammer.

'Then we hold the advantage.'

'Not for long,' said Phoenix. 'He'll soon discover you're here.'

He pointed at Eirik.

'That'll give him a clue.'

'Then we have to act quickly,' said Jon. 'It will soon be time for the final battle. Ragnarok.'

'It's time already,' said Phoenix, pointing.

Jon gasped in wonder. Until that moment the morning mist had cloaked the plain, concealing its majesty. Now, in the dawn light, his senses reeled at the scale of the stark landscape. He saw the great rainbow in the sky.

'Bifrost,' said Phoenix. 'The rainbow bridge of the gods.'

Jon stared at the ice rainbow. Bifrost arched right across the wintry sky, curving over the heads of Loki's army. Thousands of crows took flight and swept overhead.

'But how do we win?' asked Jon. 'Against that?'

'I don't know,' said Phoenix. 'The Gamesmaster has chosen this world for the final battle. These Northern myths are the gloomiest of all. The good are predestined to fall, the evil fated to destroy. All things will be put to the torch. Listen, Jon. Go back through the gate. While you're able to, while there's still time. Run the game, question your dad. Try to find something, anything we can use.'

'You can trust me,' said Jon. 'I'll find something.'

'I hope so,' said Phoenix. 'This time there are no second chances. It is the day of destiny. *This* is Ragnarok.'

3

By mid-morning the defensive preparations were made and the Berserkers were standing in anxious knots waiting for the order to take up their posts.

'I can hardly believe it,' said Halfdan, blinking away the driving sleet. 'Eirik, my most trusted comrade.'

'That wasn't Eirik,' said Phoenix. 'It was the Evil One's spirit in his body. Our enemy poisons the minds of those he seeks to control. Remember the assassin in the cellar? He had the same tattoo.'

Halfdan nodded.

'At least we have discovered the traitor. Now the lines are clearly drawn. Us against them.'

Laura viewed the hideous group at the head of the demon army. Flanking Loki were the giant wolf Fenris and Hela, goddess of the Underworld. The left side of her body was that of a young woman, pale and fair, but her right side was a rotting corpse. Behind them stood Surt the fire demon, all flame.

'Everyone is here,' said Phoenix. 'All the monsters of legend.'

Laura shook her head.

'Everyone but the gods.'

She gestured in the direction of the distant sky palace, a cluster of roofs almost hidden by the swarms of crows.

'It will be their turn soon,' said Phoenix. 'First the dark

hordes destroy the forces of Man, then they storm Asgard itself.'

'You talk as if we're beaten already,' said Laura.

Phoenix pressed his hands to his temples.

'Just look at them,' he said. 'Their ranks go on and on like an ocean. I don't know how to get us out of this one.'

'Maybe Jon will find something,' said Laura.

'Maybe,' said Phoenix.

But his voice was flat. He didn't seem to hold out much hope. What was Jon against these legions? As if to press home the huge odds against Halfdan's army, a great, nerve-shredding roar went up in the valley below. Braying horns immediately began to sound around the hilltop, calling the Berserkers to arms.

'This is it,' said Phoenix, his voice shaking.

'But what's the plan?' asked Laura.

'At this moment in time,' Phoenix answered, 'there isn't one.'

Laura was about to say something else when she screamed in terror.

'What is it?'

The ground in front of Laura had given way suddenly, leaving a huge fissure.

'Halfdan!' Phoenix roared. 'Give me some of your men. Dead-walkers. Coming from below.'

Andvar and a dozen warriors hurried to Phoenix's side and peered into the hole.

'Steady,' Andvar ordered. 'Aim your arrows into the darkness. Don't shoot until I give the command.'

They could hear the start of the assault on the Berserkers' positions, the dragons bombarding the hillside with jets of flame.

'Come on, you hell-fiends,' snarled Andvar, desperate to get back to the front line.

'I see something,' hissed Laura.

Andvar's archers drew their bowstrings.

'Steady,' said Andvar.

The word had hardly left his lips when shards of rock started flying from the hole. One of the archers, impatient for a fight, loosed his arrow.

No, came the secret speaker. *This is not your enemy.*

'Stop!' yelled Phoenix. 'Don't shoot.'

'Why?'

'I don't know. Just trust me.'

There was another shower of rocks, then a blond head appeared. Jon.

'I told you I'd find a way,' he said. 'I remembered this mountain from level eight. It stands above the gulf of Black Grief. Where Loki was held.'

'Who is this?' demanded Andvar.

Just in time, Phoenix remembered the rules of the game.

'Are you telling me you don't recognize Balder the good?'

Andvar stared.

'Not just one representative of Asgard, but two. And this second one risen from the grave!'

Jon jumped out of the hole.

'There's no time for introductions,' he said. 'By now my presence will be known. We have to act quickly. Let's go.'

He was cut off by a warning shout from Halfdan.

'Down!'

They scrambled for cover behind a row of boulders just in time to avoid a searing blast of fire from a dragon's nostrils.

'Let's get out of here,' said Laura.

'But we can't run away,' cried Phoenix. 'This is my destiny. Shouldn't I stay and fight?'

Then the secret speaker came again.

No, it told him. *Not here. Vigrid is the place where you will face your destiny.*

'So I should flee, scurry away like a coward?'

What you must do could not be achieved by a coward. Your task is to open a way for the armies of Asgard.

'I don't know if I can.'

This is my last word, young Legendeer. My time has passed. I have done everything that is in my power. The rest is up to you.

'Andreas?' said Phoenix.

But the secret speaker had fallen silent. Phoenix knew he wouldn't hear the voice again.

The rest is up to me.

'We must retreat,' he announced.

Andvar bristled.

'The Berserker does not run away,' he retorted.

'Then the Berserker is a blithering idiot!' cried Laura.

'Maybe this will wake you up,' said Phoenix. 'Just look about you, Andvar. The enemy are overrunning your defences. Is that what you want, a noble death? Noble, but quite, quite useless. You will be called on to make your sacrifice soon enough, but do it for a purpose.'

He was right about the defences. The Berserkers' hastily built fortifications were on fire, set ablaze by the swooping dragons. Through the intense heat, oblivious to the licking flames, came the dead-walkers and the fire-demons. Phoenix could see the warriors wilting under the assault, unsure whether to tackle the threat first from the front, the rear, or overhead.

'Well,' he said. 'What's it to be, Northmen?'

He was suddenly sure of himself.

'Will you choose a hero's retreat or a fool's death? Don't just stand there, Andvar. Tell me, do you trust me or not?'

The Berserkers were engaged in fierce hand-to-hand fighting. Andvar cast a glance in their direction.

'Well?' Jon demanded, standing on the edge of the hole.

'We've got to follow him,' cried Laura.

'Not without my lord Halfdan,' said Andvar stubbornly.

Phoenix grabbed his sword and raced to Halfdan's side, dashing a dead-walker out of the way with the hilt.

'There's one way out,' he panted, pointing to the hole.

Halfdan stared for a moment, then nodded as he dispatched a fire-demon with his axe.

'Fall back,' he cried. 'Archers, cover the retreat.'

As the Berserkers fled under the cover of a hail of arrows, he had a question.

'What's to stop them pursuing us into the mountain?'

'Me,' said Andvar. 'I trust you now, watchman. I'll hold them off until you get away. Who will be at my side?'

Volunteers joined him immediately.

'I was wrong about you,' said Phoenix.

'And I about you,' said Andvar.

As the last of the Berserkers tumbled past him, Phoenix smiled at Andvar.

'Into the mountain,' shouted Andvar. 'Live to fight again.'

'You!' came a voice from above.

It was Loki, sitting astride his eagle. He was snarling at Phoenix.

'You've got away many times but this will be your last!'

Phoenix searched Loki's face for the boy Adams, but he was quite transformed. A dragon appeared beside him belching a raging stream of fire. The livid mass of flame started to roll towards the hole.

'Go!' yelled Andvar, shielding himself from the flames and loosing an arrow in the direction of the hovering dragon.

Phoenix could feel every nerve and muscle shuddering with the effort. With a last look back, he followed Jon and the rest of Halfdan's band into the darkness of the mountain's tunnels. By the time the first fire-demon had penetrated them, Halfdan's army was gone.

4

Halfdan's men were defeated. They sat alone, or in silent groups. Some looked furtively into the murky passages that led from the huge cavern in which they were sitting. Phoenix glanced down at his points bracelet, a further reminder of their plight. It registered barely above zero.

'What now?' asked Laura.

Phoenix didn't meet her eyes.

'I don't know.'

He wished he could hear Andreas' voice, but it was silent. As Phoenix's knowledge and power had grown, Andreas' had faded.

I'm alone now.

The thought weighed heavily on Phoenix.

Any decisions I make are my own.

'We can't just sit here,' said Laura, nettled by his silence. 'They'll find us eventually.'

She couldn't stand still. The thought of the hell-creatures massing above made her insides crawl.

'You're right,' said Phoenix, without turning his head. 'They will.'

'Then we get them,' said Jon, eyes sparkling with enthusiasm. 'Before they get us.'

'Oh, great plan!!' cried Laura. 'In case you hadn't noticed, there are thousands of them, tens of thousands.'

Jon coloured. He suddenly felt very foolish.

Get them, thought Phoenix.

Or get him.

'No,' said Phoenix. 'Jon might have something.'

Laura threw up her arms.

'Oh, I give up! You're the one who's supposed to have the answers; you're the Legendeer. Do you remember how many of them there are?'

'How could I forget? But I'm not talking about the whole army.'

'Then what are you talking about?'

'Think about it,' said Phoenix. 'Ever since we entered the game, who have we been fighting? Demons, Northmen, Loki. That's the problem. We're fighting the monsters, not the one who's behind them. Find *him*, find the Gamesmaster, and we behead the enemy.'

'And how do we do that?' demanded Laura. 'We've played the game three times, in three different myth-worlds, but not once have we got close to him. I sometimes wonder whether he exists at all.'

'Oh, I know he exists. But you're right. So long as he is a disembodied spirit, hunting the Gamesmaster is like chasing shadows. And yet . . . I have a feeling that this time it's different. Don't you see? Look what's happening: Ragnarok, the end of days, the Evil One's triumph. It's different to the other games. Why did he choose this particular myth-world? There's a pattern to it. It's telling us something. It's the endgame. We're going to meet the Gamesmaster.'

After several moments Laura spoke.

'Are you sure?'

Phoenix nodded.

'Sure as I can be. None of this is happening by chance. The Gamesmaster lives through these worlds. The other two games told us what kind of creature he was, one that feeds off terror. They told us what his plans are. To enter our world. This game tells us *when* he is going to do it. You do understand, don't you? He has existed only as a presence, in the computer, in the game. Until now he has been a watcher, a phantom, waiting to rise. But his power has grown. Unless I'm completely mistaken his time is close. He is ready to take on physical form.'

'But how do we find him?' said Jon. 'If that's all he is, a ghostly presence, he could be anywhere.'

'Think about it,' said Phoenix. 'What's the one thing that runs through all three games? Monsters come and go, Medusa, the Minotaur, vampires, werewolves, we beat them all but we didn't win the game. Who's always there?'

Laura stated the obvious.

'Well, we are.'

'And?'

'I don't know . . . Yes, I do, Adams.'

Phoenix gave a grim smile.

'Exactly. Adams. The real terror isn't the monster at all. It's the monster inside ordinary people. Look at Adams. He began as a bullying schoolboy and was gradually taken over by the evil in the game. He's gone from being an unthinking disciple to being something utterly unfeeling and monstrous. Each time we have met him, there has been less of Adams and more of the demon. I know what's happening to him.'

Jon and Laura exchanged glances.

'We just didn't see it, Laura. All this time we've been looking for the Gamesmaster, thinking he was going to appear as himself. We missed the obvious. He must have been searching for a human vehicle. Well, he's found him. He has been growing inside Adams, slowly taking him over. It's perfect. For the Gamesmaster to come to life what does he need?'

'A body.'

'That's right. A body . . . and a mind that is easy to influence. Adams is the perfect candidate. Turning him to the dark side must have been like shaping clay. Bit by bit, the

Gamesmaster has modelled him in his own image. Now the takeover is nearly complete. We've got our final trinity. Three evil spirits in one: Adams, Loki, the Gamesmaster.'

'So he's the one we have to find,' said Jon. 'Adams, Loki, whichever you want to call him.'

Phoenix's mind was working overtime, rerunning everything that had happened in the game. He walked over to one of the passages and peered into the darkness.

'Jon, remind me how you found these tunnels.'

Jon frowned.

'You said they were near something.'

'Oh that. Yes, I recognized them from level eight. Loki was imprisoned close to here.'

'That's it,' said Phoenix. 'That was his dungeon, his place of torment. It's somewhere he has to return to, the myth demands it. Can you lead us to it?'

'I think so.'

'But surely you don't expect to find him just waiting for us?' Laura protested.

'Maybe not,' Phoenix replied. 'But it's as good a place to start as any.'

'I think this is crazy,' said Laura. 'He must be long gone.'

'Then you're not coming?'

Laura armed herself with a longbow and a quiver of arrows.

'What do you think?'

5

Phoenix followed Jon into the darkness. Laura walked beside him. She didn't speak. They had left Halfdan bemused and unsure about his next step. But he had allowed them to go without protest. They had earned his trust. For an hour, maybe longer, they trudged through the chilly gloom. It was Jon who finally broke the silence.

'Listen.'

Phoenix gave him a questioning look.

'I can hear water dripping.'

He was right. Somewhere at the end of the darkness, water was dripping. It echoed eerily.

'That has to be it. The cavern where Loki was bound in chains.'

'There's light up ahead. We've found it.'

He stepped into a vast cave. High above light filtered down through an opening, casting dappled shadows across the floor.

'See,' said Jon. 'The chains are still here. This is where he was bound. Up here . . .'

He pointed to a shelf of rock.

'This is where the serpent lay, dripping poison on his face.'

He was about to continue when a new voice echoed round the cave:

'Loki's torment obviously made a great impression on you.'

It was a female voice. Jon was the first to see her as she emerged from the shadows. He gasped out loud.

'Do I offend you, boy?' she asked.

One side of her face and body was that of a young woman, the other that of a rotting corpse. Jon turned away.

'Are you revolted by somebody who is life and death in one?' said Hela. 'Go on boy, look at me, look at my children.'

At the sound of her voice, fleshless fingers started to push up through the gaps between the stones in the floor of the cavern. Hands followed, claws of mouldering flesh. Bloodshot eyes, some dislodged from their sockets, hanging on cheeks, fixed them menacingly. Several dead-walkers were emerging out of the ground.

'Get back!' Jon warned. 'It's a trap.'

'It is indeed,' said Hela. 'And you are caught in it. Listen.'

From the passage behind them, Phoenix and Laura heard a crackling noise.

'That is the sound of Surt's fire-demons, come to see who disturbs the cave of Loki's torment. Such remarkable creatures. They are made all of flame, but they are never consumed. Only their enemies suffer the fate of immolation. Dead-walker ahead, death-maker behind. Which will you choose?'

'We came for Loki,' said Phoenix. 'Not for you.'

'But I am of his kind, flesh of his flesh,' said Hela. 'If you take a stand against him, then you make me your enemy. Besides, the Mischief-Maker has other things on his mind.'

She glanced upwards, towards the light.

'Above, on Vigrid plain.'

Instinctively Phoenix, Laura and Jon followed her gaze up towards the opening above their heads.

'That's right. Even now our legions are flushing Halfdan's Berserkers out of their hiding place. The final battle is about to begin. Maybe you can hear them whimpering and begging for mercy. You pitted yourself against the Wily One, the wolf-lord, the earth-shaker, and you have lost.'

Phoenix consulted the points bracelet. It was touching zero.

He drew his longsword and joined Jon. Laura strung the bow and made it three against the undead.

'A touching display,' said Hela. 'But quite hopeless. I must take my place on Vigrid plain. I leave you to the tender mercies of my dead-walkers. Your mission is over. I advise you to lay down your arms and accept a quick and relatively painless death.'

With that she was gone. Behind them, the three teenagers could hear the fire-demons moving closer, their blazing bodies flaring in the tunnels.

'We have to act,' said Phoenix. 'And fast.'

He held up the points bracelet for Jon and Laura to see.

'We mustn't let ourselves get caught between two enemies.'

'Meaning . . . ?'

'We know the dead-walkers. We've encountered them before. They are the lesser evil. We fight our way through them.'

Before anyone could argue, he had leapt forward and beheaded the first dead-walker with a downward slash of his sword-blade. Laura immediately loosed an arrow into a second. Jon joined them, swinging the sledgehammer. At first they seemed to be cutting a swath through the dead-walkers. Triumph showed on Jon's face.

'Just like the computer game!' he cried, his face flushed.

Gradually however the press of the undead started to force them back. The demons felt no pain, no fear. His smile vanished.

'Listen,' cried Laura. 'The fire-demons, I can hear them. They're close.'

So close she could smell them as well. Brimstone filled the air.

Jon swung his hammer in desperation but the dead-walker that had been his target clung to it and wrestled him to the ground.

'Jon!'

The creatures were pressing forward, keen to devour him. He flinched at their slimy embrace. Phoenix hacked at the closest of the creatures, then stood over Jon protectively, swinging his sword.

'Laura, use your arrows against the fire-demons. Try to hold them off.'

She loosed her arrows one after another at the shapes blazing in the darkness, but nothing stopped their advance. Her shafts merely fell to the floor as so much grey ash.

'Phoenix,' she cried, 'the quiver is almost empty, and they're still coming. I don't know how to stop them.'

Jon got to his knees and felt for his hammer. An oily, skinless hand seized his and started tugging at it. Phoenix was only just able to fend off the attacker.

'It's over, isn't it?' Jon croaked. 'We're finished.'

Phoenix shook his head furiously, but in his heart of hearts he knew it was true.

6

'Phoenix!'

The fire-demons were spilling from the tunnel behind him. Laura shot an arrow but it burned away the moment it struck its target.

'What do I do?'

'Fall back.'

Phoenix, Jon and Laura instinctively stood back to back, facing the enemies that encircled them. Their predicament had reduced them to what they were, three scared teenagers surrounded by creatures from their worst nightmares.

'Phoenix,' said Laura, 'do something.'

He glared at her.

'There's nothing I can do. What do you want, a miracle?'

And miracle is exactly what he got. As the fire-demons crouched ready to pounce, there was a shout from above.

'Take the rope!'

'Andvar!'

The giant warrior was bloodied but alive.

'How?'

'Enough questions, watchman. Take the rope.'

A knotted rope was dangling from the shelf of rock several metres above their heads. Jon and Laura seized it eagerly, while Phoenix took up the rear swinging his sword at the advancing demons.

'Now you,' cried Andvar. He was standing, feet planted apart, with the rope wrapped round his back and shoulders.

Phoenix gripped the rope and allowed himself to be hauled out of the reach of the roaring demons. Moments later he was clawing himself up onto the shelf of rock.

'How did you find us?'

'Later,' said Andvar.

Close up, his battle scars were more evident. He bore a wound which ran the length of his face and part of his left ear had been cut off.

'Are you all right?' asked Phoenix.

'I'll live to slay my share of monsters,' said Andvar. 'Follow me.'

He plunged into a tunnel. Once inside the cramped space, Jon and Laura were coughing and squinting. The smell of brimstone was overpowering. The fire-demons were coming.

'We must move fast,' said Andvar. 'Don't let me out of your sight.'

That was easier said than done. Even the faintest speck of light had disappeared. They could scarcely distinguish Andvar in the surrounding darkness. They were following a black shape in the blackness.

'Andvar?'

'I'm still here. Now, get ahead of me. The way is straight.'

'What are you going to do?' asked Laura.

'Don't worry about me, I'm not ready to sacrifice myself quite yet. I'll be with you presently.'

As they moved forward, they could hear him grunting and straining.

'What do you think he's doing?'

Then the answer was clear. There was a harsh, grating sound. He was blocking the tunnel with large rocks.

'That will hold them for a few minutes,' he said, catching up. 'Now, we are nearly free.'

Laura turned the next corner and squealed with delight. Light flooded into the tunnel.

'I never thought I'd be so glad to see snow,' she exclaimed as she stepped into the winter sunshine.

'Keep going,' said Andvar. 'Once we find a vantage point we can defend, we will rest.'

Their climb led them to an exposed peak, from which they could see Loki's army.

'Well,' Phoenix demanded, 'so how *did* you escape?'

'The dragon saved me,' said Andvar.

'You found a friendly dragon?' gasped Laura.

'Hardly,' chuckled Andvar. 'Its fiery breath killed most of my companions, but the blast hurled me down a deep shaft. I found myself falling. The only other survivor somehow evaded the demons and found me clinging to an outcrop of rock. He used this rope to save me, just as I used it to rescue you.'

'So where is he now?'

'Dead,' said Andvar with a sigh. 'The fire-demons slew him. He gave his life to save mine.'

He stared at the milling demons.

'I reached Halfdan.'

'And where is he now?'

'Still in the cavern, surrounded by Loki's fighters.'

Andvar looked into Phoenix's eyes.

'He asked me to go after you. He says you can summon the gods.'

'It's in the legend,' said Phoenix. 'I blow the Gjall horn.'

'That's it,' said Andvar. 'That's it. We must call down the gods from lofty Asgard. The seeds of this world's end were sown at its birth. Beyond the clamour of Ragnorak, Evil plans to rise.'

Phoenix looked at his friends. They knew more than Andvar how true that was. The Gamesmaster was about to take on human form. Soon he would be able to use the game to travel the worlds. He too would make the numbers dance. Nowhere would be safe from the madness that was already engulfing the nine worlds of the Northmen. The world they had left, and in which they had grown up, would be wasted just like this one.

'But what can we do to stop him?'

'Loki has eluded us,' said Phoenix. 'That bit of unfinished business will have to wait. We must return to the Berserkers. If I am to blow the Gjall horn, then we have to reach the foot of the rainbow bridge. There we will summon the gods to battle.'

Laura felt her insides lurch.

'And how do we do that?'

Phoenix turned his face to the wind. In the absence of Andreas' voice in his own head, he had to find the answer in himself.

'I will discover a way. I've got to. My whole life has been leading up to this moment.'

He stretched out his arm to indicate the battlefield.

'Ragnarok is more than a battle: it's my destiny.'

7

Finding Halfdan's Berserkers wasn't much of a challenge. As they descended the mountain, the warriors poured from a cave-mouth with a shattering roar. Phoenix's attention was drawn to the huge barrels slung between some of the horsemen's saddles. They had been carrying them ever since Skaldheim. Water barrels, he had assumed.

'Andvar found you,' said Halfdan.

'Andvar saved our lives,' said Laura.

'That was my intention,' Halfdan replied. 'Did you discover the Evil One?'

'No,' said Phoenix. 'He is too well protected. To reach him, we need the help of the gods.'

'The Gjall horn,' said Halfdan.

'Yes.'

'It lies yonder,' said Halfdan. 'There where Bifrost begins. There is a cave beneath the snow.'

'But how do we reach it?'

'We attack Loki's army. If we can draw them off, you will be able to reach the horn and summon the gods.'

'The odds are too great,' said Phoenix. 'You'll be cut to pieces.'

'There is no other way.'

'But it's such a waste,' said Laura.

'She's right,' said Phoenix.

Halfdan smiled grimly.

'It is written in the runes that out of the ashes of Ragnarok there will rise a new world, more beautiful, more hopeful, more precious than this one. If it costs our lifeblood to bring it about then the sacrifice will have been worthwhile.'

Phoenix thought of his parents watching on the computer back home. He thought of the millions of unsuspecting buyers of the game.

The sacrifice is worthwhile.

'Wait until you hear our battle-cries,' said Halfdan, 'then move quickly. Skirt their ranks and don't look for a fight.'

He looked back and waved farewell, before vanishing into the snow-glare. Phoenix noticed that Jon was trembling.

'What's wrong?'

'I don't know. It all seems so hopeless.'

'Nothing is ever hopeless,' said Phoenix. 'You heard what Halfdan said.'

The words came from part of him that had been gradually coming to life for months, ever since he first played the game.

'Ragnarok is not annihilation, but death before rebirth. The great cycle of life will turn again. The Berserkers' struggle will not have been in vain. The many worlds will be made safe. This I promise as watchman and Legendeer.'

A hoarse roar rose into the still air.

'That's Halfdan's attack,' said Phoenix.

He set off up the slope.

'He won't be fighting for nothing. I'm going to summon the gods. Who's with me?'

Jon and Laura exchanged tired looks, then trudged after him. While Phoenix, Jon and Laura struggled up the frozen mountainside, Loki's army massed in front of the Berserkers, readying themselves for the impact of the Northmen's charge. As the outnumbered warriors closed on the demon army, Loki barked his threats:

142

'A hundred miles this plain stretches in length and a hundred miles in width. Before this day is out, Halfdan, blood will stain every inch of it.'

A dismal roar greeted Loki's words, causing the earth to quake beneath the Berserkers' feet. When the battle cries finally subsided Halfdan's voice could be heard again, hoarse and almost breaking, but defiant.

'We are not afraid to die, Evil One, and know this, every one of my men who gives his life this day will take ten, a dozen – aye – even more of your odious brood with him.'

Loki raised his sword and laughed out loud.

'Look upon my demon army, Northman,' he roared, indicating the ocean of ghoulish creatures. 'You could each slay many thousands and there would be enough left to overwhelm you. My ferocious, unthinking disciples stretch to the furthest horizon.'

Halfdan knew the truth of Loki's words. A shaft of despair pierced his heart. But the Jarl of the Berserkers didn't speak again. Casting aside any concern for pain or survival, he collided with the front row of the demon army and allowed his great battle-axe Bloodletter do his talking. Andvar was at his right hand and laid about him with a terrible power, reaping the heads of the dead-walkers like corn.

'Surt,' Loki commanded. 'Let loose your fiery legions.'

The fire-demons swept towards the Berserkers. Seeing the dead-walkers stepping back to let them through, Halfdan raised a gloved hand.

'Now!'

At his command, twenty pairs of horsemen rode forward. Between them they were carrying huge barrels.

'Have you worked it out yet, Mischief-Maker?' Halfdan cried. 'Have you guessed what we have for you?'

The horsemen swept in a broad arc to the top of a rise and released the barrels which came rolling towards the fire-demons. The flaming ghouls were without fear, driven only by a soulless hatred for mortal men. But their very heartlessness and fearless battle-rage were their undoing. The moment the barrels hit the rocks that jutted everywhere out of the blanket of snow they burst open, showering the demons with icy water.

'Water,' spluttered Loki, seeing his regiment of fire extinguished in one daring movement. 'Where . . . ?'

'Why, we used what lay all around us, demon-lord,' chuckled Andvar. 'We simply melted the snow.'

The water worked like salt on slug, making the fire-demons wither and perish.

'You will pay for that,' cried Surt, their master. 'I will return with the rest of my army and destroy you.'

He jabbed a flaring hand in Halfdan's direction.

'No trick will save you then. I will tear your flesh from your bones with my own hands.'

So began a furious fight on the frozen ground: demons, goblins, dragons and Hela's living corpses swarming around the Berserkers' positions. Crows fell from the sky to peck and harry them. But Halfdan's men held their ground, his archers thinning the enemy ranks and his swordsmen and axemen hacking down wave after wave of the demon army.

'Help us, Odin!' roared the Berserkers as they steeled themselves against yet another maelstrom of screaming, clawing demons.

But their weapons were no longer scything down the enemy with the same concentrated fury and the crows' beaks left them bloodied and weary. And as they tired Loki's masses poured forward in ever-increasing numbers.

'How long can we hold them?' panted Andvar, taking a swipe at a flapping crow.

Halfdan tore open a screeching goblin with his battle-axe.

'I don't know,' he said grimly. 'May destiny grant us a little more time. We must stand our ground until the Gjall horn sounds.'

It was only then, as the Berserkers struggled to hold back the press of hideous bodies, that Loki spoke.

'Where is he, Halfdan? Where is the Legendeer, the one you call Heimdall?'

Halfdan drove his sword through yet another dead-walker.

'You'd love to know, wouldn't you, Evil One? Well, this is one Northman who will not tell you.'

Loki turned his eyes towards Bifrost.

'You've no need to, Lord of Skaldheim. I see through your ruse.'

Without another word, he sprang onto the back of his eagle. Accompanied by a flight of cawing crows, he headed for the foot of the rainbow bridge.

8

In his haste to reach the Gjall horn, Phoenix had outpaced Jon and Laura. He was far ahead of them when Laura called to him.

'Not so fast. We can't keep up.'

'You must,' Phoenix shouted back against the gusting wind. 'The battle is almost lost. There's no time to lose.'

He paused to look down at the plain below. He could just make out Halfdan's men. He admired their courage, but he had no doubt about the battle's outcome. The Berserkers were being pressed back on three sides and only Halfdan's archers were preventing them being totally surrounded. The moment their quivers were empty Loki's horde would engulf them.

'Hurry!' Phoenix yelled.

He scrambled up the slope, fighting with all his strength against the sliding snow and the driving wind. Sometimes he had to go on all fours, sometimes he sank waist-deep in the drifts

This is my destiny.

To fight him to a standstill.

'Hurry!'

He looked back to check on their progress. He was about to speak when he saw a grey-white object detach itself from the demon army and begin speeding towards him.

'What's that?'

Laura and Jon stopped to look. Phoenix set off again towards the cave. He knew what it was.

'It's him.'

'Adams?'

'Adams, Loki, whatever you want to call him now. I'm not sure there is even a trace of his human self left. They are part of the Gamesmaster now.'

The three of them drove forward, hearts hammering, their breath catching in their throats.

'Phoenix,' cried Laura. 'He's almost here.'

Phoenix didn't even glance back. He fixed his eyes on the mouth of the cave where the Gjall horn was kept.

My destiny.

With one final effort he stumbled inside. Almost immediately he felt a rush of air above his head.

'So,' said Loki from his perch on the eagle's back. 'You thought to outwit me. A mortal with the temerity to compare himself to my dark power. You have failed, Legendeer. The victory is mine.'

Phoenix saw the Gjall horn hanging from the wall.

'You will never reach it,' said Loki.

Phoenix slashed with his longsword but the eagle carried Loki out of harm's way.

'I expected better,' Loki sneered, 'from one who has thwarted me twice before.'

Phoenix's blood ran cold.

*Thwarted **me**.*

He had been right about the spirit seeking a body. This wasn't Loki, not even Adams playing a part. This was the Gamesmaster himself.

The Gamesmaster ran his hands over his chest and arms.

'I live at last. Can you imagine how long I have waited for this moment? I am *free*.'

'And Adams? What's happened to him?'

'What do you think, Legendeer? He thought he was my disciple, but I don't need anyone. His body was merely the chrysalis within which I could grow, steal through the pathways of his mind, take on life.'

Phoenix saw Laura and Jon arriving at the cave mouth.

'He welcomed me,' the Gamesmaster said, 'rejoiced as my spirit took root within every fibre of his being. He thought he was the chosen one.'

'Steve,' cried Phoenix. 'Can you still hear me? Fight back against him.'

The Gamesmaster shook his head.

'A teenage boy,' he said, 'fight me? I am the Gamesmaster, the demon-lord. Week after week I trained Adams, taught him how to think, to fight, to be. He thought I was preparing him for something great, to become my disciple. But what is greater than giving birth to your master?'

Phoenix stared into the eyes of the Evil One. They were points of cold anger. He could see nothing of Adams in them, but he had to try.

'Steve, you've got to resist. For him to come to life, you have to die. Do you understand? He is killing you. Fight him!'

His pleading was useless.

'Do you know the term "pyrrhic victory", Legendeer? One gained at too great a cost. That is all you have ever won. In the Minotaur's lair, Medusa's cave, the Vampyr's lair. What you thought were triumphs were but stepping stones to defeat. Now that I have physical form, all is possible.'

Phoenix saw Jon stealing closer until he was standing immediately beneath the hovering eagle.

'Do you understand now, Legendeer? The game is won. We are two sides of the same coin. We share a power. I too can make the numbers dance. But while I was trapped in spirit form, I was unable to use my powers. Now that I am reborn I can open the gateway between the worlds. My time has come at last.'

Phoenix was paralysed, but one person sprang into action, undeterred by the Gamesmaster's boasts. Jon seized the opportunity to hurl his sledgehammer at the underside of his mount. Startled, the eagle pitched and almost dislodged its passenger.

'You were right,' Jon cried, thrilled by the effects of his throw. 'You did make everything possible. But you're no longer a phantom.'

Phoenix stared.

What does he think he's doing?

Jon rushed forward and drove his sword into the great bird's wing. Bright blood spurted and stained the feathers. Its shriek was terrible to hear. The Gamesmaster looked startled, strangely vulnerable even. While he was fighting to regain control of the threshing eagle, Phoenix raced for the Gjall horn and sounded a blast that echoed across the frozen plain.

He had summoned the gods.

9

'I will see your blood stain the ground,' yelled the Games-master.

'Blood there will be, Gamesmaster, but it will not be ours alone. Look at the sky.'

The clouds above began to boil and the Valkyries, warrior-maidens from Valhalla, raced across the sky, their battle-shields flashing blue and black, the colour of storm and raincloud. In their wake came the Asa-gods thundering down the rainbow bridge, Bifrost. A flight of ravens led the way. Thunder bellowed as Asgard emptied its garrison, and when the armies met the crash threatened to burst the eardrums.

'It's begun,' said Phoenix. 'The final struggle.'

Then something marvellous happened. As Odin led the charge over Bifrost, the crows that had plagued the Berserkers, pecking and stabbing with their beaks, lifted their siege and wheeled away to the north.

'It's Odin,' said Phoenix. 'He has sent his ravens to reclaim the sky.'

And there were the giant birds, driving away the crows. At the sight, the Berserkers gave a roar of defiance and raced to meet the Asa-gods. Their joint charge carved a deep wedge into the ranks of the demon army and, for a brief moment, it looked as if they would carry the day with one magnificent attack. But as they hacked their way through, their onslaught slowed, bogged down in hand-to-hand fighting with the numberless enemy.

'Phoenix,' Laura began, her voice full of horror. 'Can they win?'

'I don't know,' said Phoenix.

He saw Odin, his golden helmet flashing, cutting his way towards the Fenris wolf, and Thor wielding his hammer Mjollnir. He glimpsed blind Hodur, the unwitting killer of his brother Balder, lashing out with his axe, and right beside him the giant Andvar striking at the demons.

Halfdan wiped his brow, exhausted by the effort of beating back the march of Evil that was unstoppable.

'But who cares?' said Phoenix, drawing his sword. 'We've got to help. We have to join Halfdan.'

That's when Phoenix saw the Berserkers' leader go down, crumpling beneath a mass of dead-walkers.

'No,' he cried.

But Halfdan was up, hauled to his feet by Andvar. As Phoenix, Laura and Jon struggled through the snowdrifts the clash continued.

'Rally to the raven banner,' roared Halfdan, daring any among his comrades to disagree. Seeing even the gods mired in the bloody stalemate, he was fighting a battle with his own despair, but he could hear the great banner snapping in the gale and drew strength from the sound. His cause was a worthy one.

'Make your shield-wall, warriors, stand fast and lay about the foe with sword and battle-axe,' he urged. He could feel the presence of Andvar, yet there was a great sadness in the air. Something was wrong.

'I sense that your hearts are heavy with grief, brother.'

'Our archers have fallen,' said Andvar, 'torn apart by wolves. There is no cover for our front-fighters. Our ranks are thinning, and we are completely surrounded.'

Halfdan cursed loudly and forced himself to fight even more stubbornly. He was everywhere, shoring up his faltering line. He towered above his men, helmet blazing, axe flashing. He was their inspiration.

'What keeps you going, ring-giver?' asked Andvar admiringly. 'Even the gods grow weary of the slaughter.'

'The watchman has fulfilled his destiny,' said Halfdan. 'The gods fight at our side. Hope for the future strengthens my arm.'

'There is no hope for us,' said Andvar, shearing off the head of a dead-walker. 'The odds are overwhelming.'

'Are these truly the words of my bravest comrade?' Halfdan asked. 'Look into your heart, Andvar. Destiny is a cruel master. We knew the outcome of this day before we began. None of us will live to see the good we do. But does it matter, old friend, so long as we take our stand against the enemy?'

Still the furious onslaught continued, swords and axes clashing, wolves baying and the fiery breath of the dragons hissing on the wind.

'Put aside your doubts,' said Halfdan. 'You have taken your stand against Evil. Don't give in now.'

Andvar clasped his hand.

'We die for the future,' he said.

'Never surrender,' roared Halfdan to his men, cracking the skull of a pouncing wolf. 'Fight to the last man.'

He looked around and managed a smile. His allies were true as steel. But hide it as he tried, he was plagued by doubts. Was the watchman, this Legendeer, strong enough to face the demon-lord? He wondered how the boy was faring.

Hope and apprehension filled him at the thought of the Evil One.

'Halfdan,' cried Andvar. 'Dead-Biter.'

Halfdan felt the earth pitch and roll beneath his feet like a vessel at sea.

'Where?'

'To our right.'

He heard the serpent's hiss and the thunder of Thor's hammer. An ancient prophecy was being fulfilled. God and serpent met in a furious fight. Thor finally split Dead-Biter's skull with his hammer Mjollnir. But in the moment of his victory, as Thor slew the serpent, its poisonous breath overwhelmed him.

The thunder god staggered back nine paces and died, and upon his fall a tremendous groan resonated through the defenders' ranks.

'No slackening,' yelled Halfdan, his voice hoarse. 'Arm yourselves against the horror. Fight on, for Asgard, for the future.'

He held up the raven banner so that it could be seen by all, snapping in the bitter wind. The war-god Tyr struggled against the wolf-dog Garm until both fell from their wounds. The bloody fight was resulting in the destruction of both sides.

'Are you sure your young watchman can fulfil his destiny?' panted Andvar.

'He will,' Halfdan answered, refusing to listen to his own doubts. 'He will because he must. Out of this slaughter will come renewal, a future cleansed of Evil.'

But even before the words had left his lips, the fortunes of his beleaguered men suffered another reverse. The Gamesmaster was cutting his way through the Berserkers' ranks bellowing his death-lust.

'Who will face me?' he raged, hacking at the shield-wall.

'I'll go up against you, Mischief-Maker,' said Halfdan. 'For Asgard and for the future of all.'

'Future,' snarled the Gamesmaster. 'And what future is that, Forkbeard? Look about you, your ranks are stretched to breaking point while my demon army teems about you like an ocean.'

His eyes were staring, his gaunt features streaked with blood, his hair wound into stiff horns.

'Before long you will lie at my feet, begging for your life.'

'I shall not beg, Evil One. If die I must, then I do it with a glad heart. I will rejoice to have died a hero's death.'

'Then fight,' said the Gamesmaster.

Halfdan hurled himself forward, swinging his battle-axe Bloodletter in a great arc about his head. Such was the ferocity of his attack that the Gamesmaster fell back, shaken to his core. But he soon rallied, hacking with his murderous longsword. It was Halfdan's turn to give ground, deep cuts oozing blood, weakening him. Andvar made as if to take the wounded Halfdan's place, but his war-chief pushed him aside.

'Give way, Andvar,' he said. 'This is my fight.'

Halfdan raised Bloodletter and strode forward swinging the great battle-axe.

'Do your worst, Jarl of Skaldheim,' said the Gamesmaster.

'I need no urging,' yelled Halfdan. 'I wield this weapon to seek vengeance for all my fallen brothers.'

The Gamesmaster swung his longsword but the blade clashed against Halfdan's axe-head.

'Yield,' said the Gamesmaster, 'and I will make your death a quick one.'

'Make it as slow as you like,' retorted Halfdan. 'Victory in arms will be yours, much good that it may do you.'

Halfdan smashed the battle-axe into the Gamesmaster's shield. As the axe started to fall, the Gamesmaster thrust upwards with a thin dagger he had concealed in his sleeve. The blackness of death came upon Halfdan.

'No!' cried Andvar.

With tears streaming down his cheeks he looked around the battlefield. Only a handful of Berserkers and gods were left standing, surrounded by the monstrous tide of the demon army. He saw the black dragon Nidhog, master of his kind, soaring through the air with rustling, night-black wings, blasting the earth with fire.

'The day is lost,' he murmured. 'All that is left is to die sword in hand.'

He rested a hand briefly on another warrior's shoulder.

'Afraid?' he asked.

His comrade shrugged.

'We die together in the hope of a brighter future,' the exhausted Berserker said. 'Comrades united beneath the raven banner.'

Andvar smiled, then draped the raven banner round his own shoulders and plunged into the fray. The warriors who were left followed him into the most bitter fighting.

10

Phoenix slumped to his knees. With Jon and Laura he was high above the battle. A sheer face of rock stood between them and the triumphant demon army. What could he do now that Halfdan's army was destroyed and the gods were defeated?

'What's gone wrong?' asked Jon. 'This can't be true. The Gamesmaster has won.'

'No,' said Phoenix, plunging his fists into the snow. 'It can't be true.'

'Just look down there,' cried Laura. 'Look at that carnage. We've lost. Now that the Gamesmaster has taken physical form, he can do anything.'

Phoenix stared at her.

'What did you say?'

Laura looked puzzled.

'You mean that he can do anything.'

'No,' said Phoenix. 'The other part.'

He remembered the look on the Gamesmaster's face when Jon attacked the eagle. How vulnerable he looked, how *human*.

'That's it! When he took Adams' body he took the part of Loki. You must have felt it, Jon. He can hurt, he can kill, but he can also be hurt. Now that he is flesh and blood *he can be killed*. We can destroy him.'

Laura pounced on his words.

'You mean it? There's still a chance.'

'More than a chance. If I'm right, the Gamesmaster can use the legends, but he can't break their basic rules. If he takes Loki's form, then he accepts Loki's destiny. One part of the legend remains to be fulfilled. Loki is meant to be destroyed by Heimdall. By me. But I don't know how to reach him.'

'Listen,' said Laura.

It was obvious from a deafening roar that the last warrior had fallen. Phoenix knew immediately what it meant. It was as if his heart had stopped beating.

Goodbye, men of the raven banner.

Laura seized Phoenix's wrist and looked at the points bracelet: 'This isn't right. The battle is lost, but the score is rising!'

Phoenix was about to offer an explanation when he heard a familiar voice.

'You've lost, Legendeer,' came a familiar voice. 'Soon the gateway will open and your world will lie defenceless at my feet. My demon army will pour from every computer-screen.'

It was the Gamesmaster. He had arrived fresh from the battle, surrounded by dead-walkers. He had outflanked Phoenix by climbing the slope above them before descending. The three teenagers turned with their backs to the cliff's edge. They were trapped.

'The warriors of the raven are no more,' said the Gamesmaster. 'They lie annihilated on Vigrid Plain. Soon dark Surt will unleash a sea of flame and this land will be razed. You have lost, Legendeer. The final victory is mine.'

'Is it true?' asked Laura.

Phoenix didn't answer.

'It is pointless to resist,' said the Gamesmaster. 'Your allies all lie dead. Your powers are as nought compared to mine. It is time to face facts, Legendeer. All your efforts have been futile. It's over, Legendeer.'

The Gamesmaster turned to go.

157

'Finish them,' he said to his monstrous followers.

'Finish me yourself,' said Phoenix.

'What?'

'You heard me,' said Phoenix. 'Don't leave it to them. Do it yourself. Or are you afraid of the legends? Do you still wonder whether Heimdall might defeat Loki after all?'

That the Legendeer might defeat the Gamesmaster.

'Well?'

Phoenix drew his sword.

'You're nothing,' said the Gamesmaster.

'I am the one you are destined to fight at the end of the world,' Phoenix reminded him. 'What's wrong? Afraid?'

'Of you? You have a sense of humour, Legendeer.'

The Gamesmaster drew his own sword and charged at Phoenix. Instinct jerked him back and he narrowly escaped the Evil One's sword-thrust.

'Not so easy, is it?' Phoenix taunted.

But the Gamesmaster's blade flashed again, lightning-quick, and Phoenix felt the rush of air as the killing edge narrowly missed him.

'Not so difficult either,' retorted the Gamesmaster.

He thrust downward as Phoenix's knees buckled.

'Phoenix!' cried Laura.

The Gamesmaster came on slashing with his bloodstained sword. His savage power smashed all the strength out of Phoenix's limbs. Phoenix could only raise his blade, doing his best to fend off the muscle-wasting blows. Three times the Gamesmaster's sword was held over him. Three times Phoenix squirmed out of the way. But the fourth blow hit its mark, slicing through the flesh of his underarm. He winced with pain and dropped his sword.

'And you thought I was afraid,' sneered the Gamesmaster, holding Phoenix's hair with one hand and pressing the sword's edge to his throat. 'Of *you*.'

Phoenix's fingers were clawing at the snow, trying to reach his sword.

'Say goodbye to your friends.'

But Phoenix wasn't ready for goodbyes. He remembered what Jon had said.

By taking physical form, you've made yourself vulnerable.

I can hurt you.

At long last I can hurt you.

Phoenix felt the sharp edge of the sword under his hand. There was no time to feel for the hilt. Instead he gripped the blade itself, crying out as blood spilled through his fingers.

'You're forgetting something,' he yelled, almost choking on the pain. 'This is the myth-world. We are all playing a part. You are Loki . . .'

He drove the sword into Loki's boot. He felt the electric shock of his enemy's agony.

'. . . and I am Heimdall . . .'

He threw his arms round the Gamesmaster, pulled him to the ground.

'It is my destiny to destroy you.'

Both bleeding from their wounds, they rolled down the slope to the cliff's edge.

'Phoenix,' warned Laura, 'you're too close.'

But the warning went unheeded. For a moment boy and demon fought on the very brink of disaster. Then when everything seemed frozen in time, they pitched forward and fell.

11

With Phoenix gone there was no longer a threat from the dead-walkers. The moment the Gamesmaster disappeared from sight, they became little more than statues. For several minutes Jon and Laura stood side by side staring down the sheer precipice. Their pinched faces were a mixture of horror and bewilderment. Where was Phoenix? Was he . . . ? They were both too shocked to put the question into words. In the distance they could see the demon army celebrating their victory. In their midst stood the fire-demon Surt. The two youngsters remembered the prophecy of Ragnarok.

'We've got to move,' said Laura. 'Fire. The Northland will be cleansed by fire.'

There was little time. They half-climbed, half-slid down an icy slope to the plain. Looking around cautiously, they started to pick their way gingerly through the ranks of the dead. They found the torn and broken body of Halfdan Forkbeard first. Andvar was away to their right.

'What a waste,' said Laura. Then she called out, 'Phoenix.'

There was no reply.

'You have to be here,' she said.

She looked at the precipice from which Phoenix and the Gamesmaster had plunged.

'You've got to be.'

She searched ever more feverishly and impatiently, stepping

over the corpses of men and demons alike. She moved in circular sweeps, but still there was no sign.

'Where are you?'

He should be here, either standing waiting for them, or broken under the raven sky.

'Phoenix!'

In the distance, the burning had begun. A sea of red flame was sweeping across the battlefield. Jon turned to look.

'The dusk of the gods,' he murmured.

Everything felt so final. Were they going to perish here too? Were there no winners on this terrible plain?

'Phoenix, please.'

She could hear the roar of the great fire, the crackle of the bodies as they were consumed. Every instinct was telling her to get away, to flee for her life. Then she saw it, the body of the Gamesmaster. She looked down at his face. The features were softer now. She could see Adams in them.

'But where's Phoenix?'

She searched frantically, but there was no body.

'Laura,' Jon yelled, his voice flying up on the wind. 'We've got to go.'

'I can't leave without him,' Laura said tearfully.

'There's nothing more we can do,' said Jon. 'We've just got to hope Phoenix made it. The game is won. Somewhere the gateway must be open, I just know it. Do you understand? We can go home. We've just got to find it. If we stay here we'll be killed.'

The fire was coming closer.

'We have to go now. We've got to run.'

'Run, run, run,' echoed the hills.

The prophecy had come true. The sun was darkening at high noon, the heavens and the earth had turned red with blood. The moon was lost in darkness and the stars had vanished from the sky. Fire was enveloping the land, black smoke wreathing the mountain tops.

'The gateway, Laura,' said Jon. 'We have to find it.'

'The end has come,' Laura murmured. 'Ragnarok.'

But it was the end only of this world.

'Look,' cried Jon. 'There, the gateway is open.'

There it was, a golden portal of light imprinted with silver numerals.

'We've done it, Laura. We can go home.'

Laura looked at the gateway, then at the tidal wave of roaring fire. She examined the footprints on the snow in front of the gateway. Did they belong to Phoenix? Had he opened it for her? And if so, where was he now?

'What about Phoenix?'

'We have to go,' said Jon. 'If he's alive he'll find us.'

The fire was almost upon them. Acrid smoke was stinging Laura's eyes and clogging he throat. She cast one more desperate glance over the carnage of the battlefield, then her mind was made up.

'Let's go home,' she said.

12

Two weeks later Laura Osibona was crossing the road when she saw a familiar figure. Her heart missed a beat.

'Phoenix, is that you?'

She hurried to the kerb, hesitated for a moment, then rushed to him, throwing her arms round him and clinging to him.

'Phoenix, you're alive!'

She could hardly believe her eyes. So much had happened in the last fortnight: her parents' endless questions, the police investigation, the publicity. Everybody was talking about Phoenix's disappearance, and linking it to that of Steve Adams. Each day that had passed had made her more certain he was dead.

'Does this mean you're back?'

Phoenix smiled thinly.

'For good? No.'

'Then why are you here?'

'I want you to do something for me.'

'Of course, anything.'

'I want you to call on Mum and Dad, to tell them you've seen me and that I'm all right.'

Laura frowned.

'But why not tell them yourself?'

Phoenix shook his head.

'I'm not putting them or myself through it. They'd only beg

me to stay. It would be too upsetting for us all. No, it's better this way.'

'But Phoenix, it's crazy. What's stopping you from coming home?'

'The Gamesmaster.'

They walked together through the trees.

'The Gamesmaster? But he's dead. I saw his body. We won, didn't we?'

Phoenix watched a sheet of newspaper skipping down the path, blown by the wind.

'Did we?'

'Of course we did. Magna-com has gone out of business, completely bankrupt. It's caused quite a scandal. *Warriors of the Raven* never made it to the market. *The Legendeer* trilogy has been withdrawn from the shelves. It's over, Phoenix, it really is.'

Phoenix stopped and turned towards her. He shook his head.

'No, it isn't over.'

'What do you mean?'

'Just that. The body you saw was Adams. Remember what the Gamesmaster said. Steve was a vehicle, something he used. All I did was destroy the body. The spirit lives.'

'I don't believe it. I won't. He died in that fall.'

'Who are you trying to convince?' asked Phoenix. 'Yourself?'

Laura held his hands.

'You can't throw your life away on a wild goose chase. I tell you, he's gone. Phoenix, you've won.'

His face was hard, impenetrable. She knew immediately that her words were falling on deaf ears.

'No, he's out there somewhere, preparing.'

He was already looking past her, as if fixing his attention on a world beyond her.

'But where, Phoenix, where have you been?'

'You should see it, Laura. So many worlds, they just go on and on. Every myth, every legend, every strange story that has haunted the human imagination, they exist. Anything can happen, any dream can come true. It isn't just nightmares any more. It's so wonderful.'

He leaned his forehead against hers for a moment.

'You could come with me. I could show you.'

Laura smiled:

'This isn't about the Gamesmaster, is it? It's about you as well. You don't *want* to come home.'

She gave him a look that cut through him like a knife, then gently withdrew her hands.

'You've made your choice, Phoenix. I think we always knew what it would be. But I belong here. This is my world.'

Phoenix lowered his eyes.

'It's not mine, Laura. It never was. For me and Andreas there was only ever one choice, one destiny. I was always going to leave it one day. For the first time in my life, I feel like I belong.'

'So you've made up your mind then, you're not coming back?'

'No, Laura, I'm not coming back. I know Mum and Dad are upset, but deep down I think they knew all along. It was my destiny.'

There seemed to be a great distance between them. The old familiarity was gone, replaced by a curious awkwardness, as if they were strangers.

'Has it been hard?' Phoenix asked. 'Trying to explain what happened?'

'The police have asked a lot of questions about your disappearance. But they can't prove foul play. They're completely baffled by the whole thing.'

'That's all I needed to know,' said Phoenix. 'So long as everybody is safe.'

165

'Yes, Phoenix, we're safe.'

There was an uncomfortable silence, then Laura spoke again.

'When you say you're not coming back, does that mean ever?'

Phoenix took a few steps back from her.

'Surely you know the answer to that. If I'm right, and the Gamesmaster is still alive I have to find him and put an end to him for good and all.'

Laura nodded.

'So this is the last time I will ever see you?'

'That's right. The last time.'

'Be happy then, Phoenix, and don't forget me.'

Phoenix laughed.

'After what we went through together, how could I? Listen, I have to go. You will see my parents, won't you?'

'Of course I will.'

'Thanks, it means a lot to me.'

He conjured the numbers in the air and stood in front of the gateway.

'You're sure you can't come?'

Laura shook her head.

'I'm sure.'

'Then it's goodbye.'

Without another word, he stepped into the golden portal and was gone.

'Goodbye, Phoenix,' said Laura. 'Goodbye, Legendeer.'

Also by Alan Gibbons

The Shadow of the Minotaur

'Real life' or the death defying adventures of the Greek myths, with their heroes and monsters, daring deeds and narrow escapes – which would you choose?

For Phoenix it's easy. He hates his new home and the new school where he is bullied. He's embarrassed by his computer geek dad. But when he logs on to The Legendeer, the game his dad is working on, he can be a hero. He is Theseus fighting the terrifying Minotaur, or Perseus battling with snake-haired Medusa.

The trouble is The Legendeer is more than just a game. Play it if you dare.

Vampyr Legion

What if there are real worlds where our nightmares live and wait for us?

Phoenix has found one and it's alive. Armies of bloodsucking vampyrs and terrifying werewolves, the creatures of our darkest dreams, are poised to invade our world.

But Phoenix has encountered the creator of *Vampyr Legion*, the evil Gamesmaster, before and knows that this deadly computer game is for real – he must win or never come back.

The Edge

Danny is a boy on the edge. A boy teetering on the brink of no return, living in fear.

Cathy is his mother. She's been broken by fear.

Chris Kane is fear – and they belong to him.

But one day they escape. They're looking for freedom, for the promised land where they can start really living. Instead they find prejudice, and danger of another kind.

Uncompromising and disturbing, but utterly readable, Alan Gibbons' latest novel positively crackles with tension as he writes about a mother and her son desperate to start a new life.

'This is a fast and compelling "must read" that is disturbing in ways that are bound to make teenagers confront important issues like racism and endemic violence. I can't recommend it highly enough.'
Books for Keeps

Ganging Up

John and Gerry have always been friends, brought together by their passion for football. Then Gerry's dad loses his job and everything turns sour. The two boys had always steered clear of the gangs at school, but Gerry gets drawn in and now he and John find themselves standing on opposite sides.

Set in a tough inner city Liverpool estate, this is a story about friendships, rivalries and survival played out at school and on the football field.

Caught in the Crossfire

'You know what happens to people like you? You get hit in the crossfire.'

Shockwaves sweep the world in the aftermath of 11 September. The Patriotic League barely need an excuse in their fight to get Britain back for the British, but this is chillingly perfect.

Rabia and Tahir are British Muslims, Daz and Jason are out looking for trouble, Mike and Liam are brothers on dfferent sides. None of them will escape unscarred from the terrifying and tragic events which will weave their lives together.

Marking a new dimension in his writing on race, riots and real life, *Caught in the Crossfire* is an unforgettable novel that Alan Gibbons needed to write.

'Gibbons' writing often addresses worrying issues of social justice but never as powerfully as in this novel . . . the writing – short, sharp pieces that take us into the mind of each character – is accessible and compulsive.'

Wendy Cooling, *The Bookseller*

The Dark Beneath

'Today I shot the girl I love.'

GCSEs are over and sixteen-year-old Imogen is looking forward to a perfect, lazy English summer. But her world is turned upside down by three refugees, all hiding from life. Anthony is fourteen, already an outcast, bullied and shunned by his peers. Farid is an asylum seeker from Afghanistan, who has travelled across continents seeking peace. And Gordon Craig is a bitter, lonely man. Imogen knows all of them, but she doesn't know how dangerous they are. Being part of their lives could cost Imogen her own.

Supercharged with tension and drama, Alan Gibbon's novel is about what happens when the fabric of normality is ripped apart exposing the terrifying dark beneath.

The Lost Boys' Appreciation Society

Something was wrong. The anger-flash had drained out of Dad's face, replaced by a blank pallor.

Like disbelief . . .

When Mum was killed in a car crash our lives were wrecked too.

Gary, John and Dad are lost without Mum. Gary is only 14 and goes seriously off the rails, teetering on the brink of being on the wrong side of the law. John is wrestling with GCSEs and his first romance – but he's carrying the burden of trying to cope with Gary and Dad at the same time. And they're all living with the memories of someone they can never replace.

'Gibbons . . . writes with passionate conviction.'
Gillian Cross, *Guardian*